BAT OUT OF SPELL

An Elemental Witches of Eternal Springs Cozy Mystery

AMANDA M. LEE

WinchesterShaw Publications

Copyright © 2018 by Amanda M. Lee

All rights reserved.

No part of this book may be reproduced in any form or by any electronic or mechanical means, including information storage and retrieval systems, without written permission from the author, except for the use of brief quotations in a book review.

❦ Created with Vellum

One

"You'd better hope I don't find you!"

I tilted my head to the side, my ears trained for any hint of sound, and narrowed my eyes to glittering blue slits as I waited for the inevitable taunt. Even though I believed there was a chance he'd learn his lesson (and we're talking every time, not just once), I always turned out to be wrong. This wouldn't be the time things changed, yet still I waited.

Then it happened.

Cackle, cackle, cackle.

Zoom, zoom, zoom.

I ducked as a small creature barely skirted my scalp and then disappeared somewhere into the bowels of the house. I smacked my hands protectively to the top of my head and let loose a screech that bounced off the walls with enough force to cause the hooting beast I was convinced hid in the hallway, poised to strike, to stop the chattering he enjoyed making when he wanted my brain to explode.

I wanted to be calm. Things would end better if calmness reigned supreme. That's simply not how I operate, though.

"Swoops!" I yelled loud enough that I was certain the neighbors heard. Even though Eternal Springs is big enough that neighbors aren't piled on top of each other – there is actual space between houses, which benefitted me a great deal – I have one of those voices that carries. I like to think of it as uniquely attention-grabbing. Others have told me it's like nails on a chalkboard overlaid with noisy chewing all the while surrounded by the dulcet sounds of some insipid boy band crooning a pop ballad.

This is one of those times I agreed to disagree with people. That happens a lot, by the way.

I checked the spot on my scalp where I was convinced I was missing hair and stomped my foot to get my annoying roommate's attention. Sure, Swoops isn't a normal roommate. He isn't even a normal pet. Most people have cute kittens or dopey dogs to dote on. Me, I have a bat.

No, you heard that right, Swoops is a bat. Don't worry, I litter trained him. He doesn't do his business in the house or anything. Of course, that's not what most people cringe at when they find out I have a pet bat. The first thing I always hear is, "Aren't you afraid of rabies?"

For the record, no. I, Skye Thornton, am not afraid of rabies. Swoops is clean. Okay, he isn't *clean* clean, but he's not rabies infested or sleep-in-his-own-feces addled or anything. He eats like a messy toddler and takes his humor cues from teenage boys (which means he enjoys fart jokes and a good grope when he thinks he can mess with someone). Instead of a bat, it's almost as if I have an annoying male child that I never wanted. Too bad I can't leave him at a fire station under one of those safe haven laws. That would make my life so much easier.

"If you stole my hair again we're going to have words," I barked, planting my hands on my hips and waiting for Swoops to make an appearance. He's a dramatic little thing, all theatrical entrances and extended pauses so I know he really means business. The gluttonous scamp is such a rampant over-actor that he could headline a soap opera ... or an episode of one of those Real Housewives of Places I Never Want to Live programs.

How did I end up with a bat as a pet? That's a good question. It turns out he's my familiar. Oh, yeah, I'm a witch. Did I fail to mention that? The word "witch" can mean different things to different people, so it's probably good to clarify exactly what type of witch I am.

I am not the type who enchants shoes or has a wart on the end of my nose. I can fly around on a broom, though. I shunned the cliché for years, refusing to be *that* person. No one likes *that* person. Then I finally broke down and read Harry Potter in high school and I became *that* person. You know what? Now I'm officially fine being *that* person.

I didn't grow up in Eternal Springs — that's the name of this ridiculously small island I'm forced to call home — but I was sent here to make sure I got the very best education possible. That meant being taught with other witches. That meant making friends with other witches. And, ultimately, when the school burned down due to negligence on the part of the people who were supposed to be watching the bridge to the other side — I'm not saying I was at fault as much as distracted by others, and I still maintain they were to blame and I was an innocent bystander caught up in a situation I didn't create — I was part of the team who was left behind to continuously clean up the mess of a fallen ideal.

I know. I think it sounds stupid, too. That doesn't change the fact that I'm stuck on an island off the New Jersey shore — I mean, why couldn't we at least be in a good location, like near Florida or even one of the Carolinas I hear so much about but never get to visit? And I can't leave until there's absolutely no threat to Eternal Springs. Who knows when that will be? It could be never.

"I don't have time for you now, Swoops," I called out as I picked my way through the house. I needed to fill my travel mug with coffee if I expected to make it through my first assignment of the day. In addition to being one of Eternal Springs' witchy saviors (I'm one of four, but more on that later), I'm also the owner ... and lone reporter ... and lone layout person (although I do have occasional temporary help from time to time) for The Town Croaker, Eternal Springs' only newspaper. That means I have to cover every mundane thing that happens on the island, including the opening of a new wing at the spa. I know, exciting stuff.

I heard Swoops chattering as he zoomed through the house in my wake. He recognized I was heading for the kitchen, which just so happened to be his favorite room in the house, and whatever mayhem he initially had planned fell by the wayside at the prospect of food.

"I'm not feeding you," I called out as I filled the basin with water and selected a nice French roast pod for my morning caffeine rush. "You were up until two last night eating popcorn. You left bits of it all over the house, including in my bed. That means I'll have to vacuum when I get home this afternoon. You know how I feel about domestic chores."

The chattering was much closer this time and when I shifted my eyes to the top of the refrigerator I found Swoops watching me with pitiful eyes.

"I'm not feeding you," I repeated. "You're fat. Bats aren't supposed to be fat. You need to go on a diet. I don't want to be the only witch in town with a fat familiar."

Swoops feigned clutching at his chest as he staggered on top of the refrigerator. His steps were so exaggerated he almost looked drunk.

Must have food. Will die without it.

Swoops can't talk, but because he's my familiar I can read his mind. He can also read mine. I'm not comfortable with either ... and it's not just because I enjoy looking at the occasional naughty photograph on the internet (when it works, that is).

"You're not going to die." I made a face as I glared at him. "You ate your weight in popcorn last night. You also ate SpaghettiOs, an apple, a bag of Rolos and a jar of pickled okra, although I have no idea where that came from because I certainly didn't buy it."

Am circling the drain.

Swoops looked pitiful as he blinked his big eyes. I knew he was faking, but I couldn't hold out.

"Fine." I blew out a sigh as I stomped to the refrigerator and grabbed a fresh apple from the crisper. "Here." I planted the apple on top of the refrigerator and cocked an eyebrow when Swoops curled his lip. No, really, he looked like Elvis. "What's wrong?"

Corned beef hash.

Ugh. I had to be the only witch in the world whose familiar was addicted to corned beef hash. I shook my head. "No. I don't have time. I have to be at the spa in forty minutes."

Corned beef hash.

I stared hard into Swoops' eyes. I swear the little moppet actually looked as if he was going to cry. I tried one more time to beat a hasty retreat without having to cook him breakfast. I had to be strong. "I can't be late. You know how Kenna is when I'm late."

Kenna Byrne, one of my witch sisters, was the most anal-retentive schedule Nazi who ever walked the planet. If I was even five seconds late she would know. Worse than that, she'd jot it down in that little appointment book she carries and then bring it up the next five times I ran into her. No, I couldn't deal with that. She was worse than a pathetic Swoops any day of the week.

"I have to go." I slapped the cover on my coffee mug and moved toward the door. "I'll make you corned beef hash later."

When I risked a glance over my shoulder I found Swoops was no longer acting pathetic and weepy. Instead, he'd turned belligerent and his stance promised payback later.

"Don't even start," I warned.

Swoops merely sneered as he left his perch and headed toward the hallway. *Oh, it's on.*

That's exactly what I was afraid of.

THE ETERNAL SPRINGS SPA and Resort was the island's lone claim to fame after the loss of the school thirteen years earlier. I was a senior at the time the school succumbed to the biggest fire to ever hit the area, so I had to finish out my education in public school. That meant I knew the locals, including August "Augie" Taylor, the world's biggest pain in the keister, who just happened to be head of security at the resort.

I held out my press badge, which was homemade and enhanced with glitter, to the faceless security drone at the entrance after I parked my pink Vespa in the lot. Oh, yeah, there are no cars on Eternal Springs. The tourism board believes they take away from the island's natural ambiance (as if that's a real thing) so everyone drives scooters and golf carts. Even when it snows, so you can imagine what that's like as golf carts skid into ditches and the world comes to an end when three inches of fluff falls like clockwork every Christmas.

I kept my gaze on Augie and ignored the security guard

studying my credentials. If I could make it to the news conference without having to speak to him my day would vastly improve. The second he shifted in my direction, though, I knew that was not to be.

"That doesn't look official." The security guard, who I'd never seen before, had the name "Brad" embroidered on his shirt. He was clearly new, which meant he was doomed to be slow on the uptake when it came to the reality of Eternal Springs.

That was always a bummer.

"It's official, Brad," I shot back. "I'm with The Town Croaker."

Brad uncomfortably shifted from one foot to the other. "It has pink glitter on it."

I could blame Swoops for that. The last time he got angry with my culinary skills he decided to pay me back by spreading pink glitter around the house. He dusted it on everything, including my press pass. He also managed to drop some in my shampoo and underwear drawer. He truly was a monster when he wanted to be. "It's still official."

"I need to check with my boss."

"Wait." The word was barely out of my mouth before Brad called to Augie. My high school nemesis seemed to be expecting the cry for help because he added a little swagger to his step as he joined us.

"What seems to be the problem, Agent Lockwood?"

Agent Lockwood? That had to be a joke. "Why are you calling him 'agent?' He's a security guard." The question was out of my mouth before I remembered that I didn't want to engage in mindless conversation with a guy who made my skin itch because he was so snarky. Don't get me wrong, I'm a big fan of snark. But I much prefer it when I'm the one doling it out.

"That's his title," Augie replied simply, accepting the press pass from Brad and smirking. "Nice glitter."

"Thank you. He's not an agent, though. He's a rent-a-cop."

Augie's smile slipped. "He's an agent of Eternal Springs Spa and Resort."

Was that supposed to impress me? "Whatever." I didn't bother to hide my eye roll. "Can you clear me through? I'm going to be late for the news conference. Kenna will be all over me if that happens."

"Yes, well, I don't pretend to understand your relationship with the other girls from your school." Augie handed back the press pass. "That really does look unprofessional."

"So does wearing black socks with sandals." I gestured toward his feet. "Do you really want to get in a battle about who is more unprofessional?"

Augie shrugged. "We've fought about more juvenile things than that."

He wasn't wrong. "I have to get going. I'm running late."

"Whose fault is that?"

Oh, now he was just trying to get under my skin. He was like a tick. He wanted to suck my blood and give me whatever the personality equivalent of Lyme disease is. "Augie, I'm not joking. I have to get over there. If I'm late I'll be in a boatload of trouble."

Instead of letting me through, Augie narrowed his eyes. "August. My name is August."

Whoops. I always forgot he hated being called Augie. I was hardly the only one on the island to refer to him by that moniker. His high school nickname had stuck. He wanted to be called "August" because it sounded more professional. I mostly ignored his request, but because I was running late that would've been a prime way to butter him up.

Ah, next time. "I'm sorry." I didn't mean it. Not even a

little. "I'm simply frazzled. It's been a long morning and it's not even eight yet."

Augie heaved out a sigh, resigned. "I would torture you and not let you through, but the resort owners are relying on coverage for the big event." He swept out his left arm and pointed toward the new building, which was so white it gleamed under the early morning sun. "You should probably get over there."

"Great." I started striding in that direction.

"And don't wander!" Augie yelled to my back. "You have a tendency to wander and stick your nose into places it doesn't belong."

I would've argued the point, but I didn't have time and, well, he was right. I'm a wanderer and busybody. I'm not sorry about either.

I tried to push Augie's attitude and words out of my mind as I increased my pace to the point I was almost running. I saw Kenna's black hair from five hundred yards and knew she was probably already melting down. That's her way. If the slightest thing went wrong and her schedule was thrown off by as little as thirty seconds she'd make me pay in unfathomable ways. Her mind was so warped she'd make Swoops' glitter bomb attack look like child's play.

I was so lost in thought – and determined to be in my seat before the clock rolled over to eight – I decided to cut through a small patch of foliage. We're talking low bushes and flowers that I can easily jump over, so it's not as if I planned to trample anything. That didn't exactly happen, though.

Instead of breezing through the area, gracefully leaping over the bushes and planting myself in a chair so I could pretend I'd been there the entire time I tripped over my own feet and sprawled into the bushes. I landed hard enough that

I whimpered ... and then made a face when I realized my tailbone was vibrating.

"Graceful," Kenna snarked, her business suit immaculate as she watched me from fifty feet away.

Great. She was going to punish me regardless. Why did I bother to run? "Yes, well, I almost became an ice dancer rather than a reporter," I said, planting my hand on the ground to give myself leverage to stand, frowning when I realized something was under me. "I think I might have missed my calling."

I shifted to stare at the large item sticking out from beneath the bush's green boughs and almost choked on my own tongue when I realized I was staring into a pair of lifeless eyes. They were green ... and glazed ... and emanating from a woman who was very clearly dead.

Uh-oh. It seemed my morning was going to take another turn ... and it was one none of us needed.

"Well, fiddlesticks."

Two

Eternal Springs Spa and Resort is famous for several things. The biggie is the mud pits. I've never understood why anyone would want to sit in mud — I mean, it's wet and dirty, people — but it's a thing and the resort is almost always packed. The resort is the only way the island can sustain itself, so I'm grudgingly respectful of the facility and the people who run it.

Its other claim to fame is its plastic surgery wing. People come from far and wide for face time with the resort's gaggle of world-renowned doctors. Why was that important in the wake of me stumbling over a dead body? Because once the woman was identified her appearance garnered a few questions.

"This is marvelous work." Dr. Abigail Marley crouched next to the body, a medical bag beside her, and made clucking sounds with her tongue. "Absolutely phenomenal! She's fifty, but looks thirty. I did a great job."

It took everything I had not to roll my eyes — and maybe smack her upside the head — as I watched her toil over the body. "That's great. I mean ... truly spectacular. Do you want to focus on something more important, though? I'm thinking how she died might be a good place to start."

Abigail never liked me. In truth, I don't think she likes anyone but herself. The look she shot me now was straight out of an old *Dynasty* episode ... and I should know because I've been binge watching the show after finding old DVDs at a town rummage sale. Hey, when you're stuck on an island with spotty internet and cable service you take your entertainment where you can get it.

"Did you say something, Skye?"

Her dismissive tone set my teeth on edge. "Yes. I said ... ."

Kenna extended a hand to quiet me. Her expression suggested that I would be in line for a whopping case of payback if I didn't bite my tongue. "I think what Skye is asking is how did this particular woman end up in the bushes?"

That was only half of what I was asking. "And how did she die," I added, refusing to cringe when Kenna burned holes into the side of my face with her laser stare of death.

"I'm more interested in who she is." Augie was all business as he kneeled and peered closer at the woman's face. "Is she one of ours?"

"I think Abigail already answered that for you," I volunteered. "She said she had great work done. The best. Tremendous. A-number-one. Why else would she be here if it wasn't for a freshening treatment?"

I hated that term. *Freshening treatment.* That's what the resort bigwigs call it, though, and because tourism is important I'd forced myself to start referring to it in the exact same manner. I was a team player, after all. Oh, who am I kidding? The only team I want to be on is the one expected to gold medal at the Sarcastic Olympics of 2019.

"I was merely asking a question," Augie snapped, his temper ratcheting up a notch. I always had a negative effect on his patience. "You shouldn't even be involved in this conversation. Can someone tell me why she's here?"

"Because Skye tripped over her and we need her cooperation to present this story in a positive manner," Kenna shot back. "Let's not make things worse than they have to be."

"Yeah, Augie." I made a face behind Kenna's back, sticking out my tongue and miming a vulgar act. I knew it would infuriate Augie and I was nothing if not consistent when it came to my efforts to irritate. "Let's not make things worse."

"You're such a pain," Augie muttered, shaking his head.

"She's definitely a pain," Abigail agreed, her tone clipped. "But she's not wrong. This woman is a regular. She comes several times a year. Her name is Blair Whitney."

Blair Whitney. That sounded about right for a fifty-year-old who looked thirty and had a helmet for hair. Yes, even in death Blair Whitney's hair-sprayed monstrosity remained completely immovable. Since Kenna's witchy powers revolved around fire, it was probably best not to stir her temper because then we would find ourselves mired in an incident ... and not a good one. Of course, we were already mired in an incident thanks to the body, but if I'd learned anything over my thirteen years in exile on this stupid island it's that things could always get worse.

"See. I was right." I folded my arms across my chest. "Ha."

"You're going to get it later," Kenna groused under her breath.

Hmm. It wasn't even nine yet and I'd already amassed two threats. It was going to be a good day.

"She probably just tripped or something," Abigail noted as she dug in her medical bag. "I don't see any obvious injuries."

Was she blind? This is what happens when you live in a place that's so small that a plastic surgeon at a resort doubles as the medical examiner. I mean ... seriously. "What about that big knot on the back of her head?" I challenged. "You know, the one with the blood. It's right there. I can see it through that helmet doubling as hair."

"Knot?" Abigail knit her eyebrows. "I ... oh, you're right."

"What was your first clue?"

Abigail ignored my sarcasm and leaned across the body to study the wound. I wasn't a forensics expert or anything, but I'd watched enough crime procedurals to know that was a bad idea.

"You're screwing with the evidence," I complained, looking to Kenna for help.

"I'm the medical examiner. I know how to preserve evidence."

"If you knew how to preserve evidence you wouldn't be pressing your boobs against the victim's chest and transferring your DNA to the body."

Abigail's expression darkened. "Are you telling me how to do my job?"

I thought that was rather obvious. "Yes!"

"Knock it off, Skye." Kenna gripped my elbow — her perfectly manicured fingernails digging into the soft flesh there — and tugged me away from the scene. "I think you've said enough for one day."

I was nowhere near done, but if she wanted to talk in private, I was all for it. "Sure. Great. Awesome."

Kenna wrinkled her nose. "I hate it when you use that tone."

"And I hate it when you mention my tone."

"And I hate it when you complain about me mentioning your tone." Kenna's pretty face turned dark. "Why must you always make things so difficult?"

"That's how I roll."

"Whatever." She exhaled heavily — a calming technique I'm sure she learned from the yoga classes I imagined she attended. Granted, I had no direct knowledge of her participating in the daily yoga classes at the spa, but that's how I often pictured her. You would think that we'd be the best of friends after surviving the "incident" together, bonding through tragedy and the like, but you'd be wrong. Our relationship was more tenuous. That said, we had each other's backs in times of tumult because ... well ... we always managed to find trouble. For example, it helped to have backup when you had to dislodge a demented mermaid from the area beneath the dock because she was gnawing on feet. That really happened. She snagged a few toes before we managed to vanquish her. Some of the locals still believe there was a very picky shark lurking around the shallows, threatening to forever alter their balance in a demented game of *This Little Piggy*.

"We need to keep calm." Kenna was the pragmatic sort. As the head of the tourism board, she kind of had to be. She wasn't allowed to melt down in public or hide away in bed for a week with nothing but a pet bat and corned beef hash when the mood struck. No, she always had to be "on." I felt sorry for her.

"I am calm." That was mostly true. I was calm-ish. "I still think it's ridiculous that we have a plastic surgeon who looks like a human Barbie doll acting as our medical examiner."

"She is going a little overboard with the plastic surgery of late," Kenna reluctantly agreed, shaking her head. "She looks kind of frozen, as if she can't make an expression."

Oh, that was putting it diplomatically. "She looks like that crazy woman who had so much plastic surgery she now resembles a cat."

"She's not that bad."

"She's close."

"She's simply ... enthusiastic about what she does for a living," Kenna offered. "I think you're too hard on her."

Translation: Stop making a scene because I need to think about how to spin this. I could read Kenna fairly well and I knew that was her biggest concern. "I promise not to be hard on her. Happy?" I moved to rejoin the small group still crowded around Blair Whitney, but Kenna intercepted me before I could escape. It was almost as if she read my mind and intuited what I had planned. Sadly, that was a possibility. She knew me as well as I knew her. "Oh, come on."

"We're not done talking." Kenna was firm. "You can't just take over a crime scene because you want to be in charge."

"I think you're confusing me with you."

"I think you're being a pain because you tripped over a body and it's stirred you up," Kenna corrected.

"I am not stirred up."

"You always get stirred up."

I was going to stir her up if she wasn't careful, and then we would have a fire to contend with, too. How would she like that?

"Now, we need to keep our heads about us." Kenna adopted a reasonable persona, as if I were the nutty one and she was perfect. That's always how she is. I hated it. "We have to figure out what happened to this woman and not let the guests panic. If they panic, they're likely to leave. That means they won't spend money in town. Do you want that?"

"I haven't decided yet."

Kenna ignored my response. "You need to make sure you don't play this up too much in your article. You're here to cover the opening of the new wing. That's where your focus should be."

She had to be kidding. "If you expect me to ignore a dead body, you're crazier than our medical examiner."

"I don't expect you to ignore it. I simply don't want you making it the focus."

"Yeah, well, we'll see. I ... ." Whatever I was about to say died on my lips when a familiar golf cart – one with a knit purple cozy covering the hood and a matching awning – pulled to a stop about thirty feet away. The man behind the wheel was the last person I wanted to see. "Oh, geez!"

Kenna followed my gaze, her lips twisting into a dark expression. "We should've known he would show up."

Yes, we definitely should've known that Barnaby Sterling Montgomery, or Buddy to the great unwashed, would show up. He was the mayor, after all. That also made him the chief of police, the senior center president, the water department chief and the guy who mowed the lone median in the center of the downtown area. Okay, he didn't mow it. His long-suffering wife Mitzi did. She never left his side, although she clearly hated him as much as everybody else because she spent all her time sitting in the passenger seat of his golf cart knitting. Sometimes – and I swear this is true – she loses her ability to cover her real feelings and I can see that she wants to stab her husband with those metal needles she's always working. I can't blame her. We all want to stab Buddy.

Buddy hefted his expansive girth out of the golf cart – I'd heard through the grapevine they had to design a special unit for him because his gut was so big he couldn't fit in a standard cart. No, seriously. I don't like weight shaming people – no one but Buddy, really – but he had to weigh six-hundred pounds. I often worried he would roll over in his sleep and crush his tiny wife. Of course, that could be why she carried the knitting needles. Maybe she understood there would come a time when she had to stab him to ensure her survival.

"Don't panic, folks."

I glanced around. No one was even close to panicking.

"I'm here to perform my usual magic and fix things. What do we have here?" Buddy clomped closer to Augie and Abigail, his expression unreadable as he studied the body on the ground. He didn't look surprised, or especially sympathetic, but he was often enigmatic. Er, well, unless there was cake involved. And ribs. And sometimes cornbread. When you combined all three, he was positively effusive.

"She's dead," Abigail announced. "She was struck on the back of the head."

"Oh, that's terrible," Mitzi tittered. She was so small she almost always seemed invisible next to her husband. She would've made a fine spy if the CIA ever decided to take up shop in Eternal Springs. "Did she fall?"

"We can't be sure," Augie replied, straightening to shake Buddy's hand. Even though Augie wasn't a real cop he fancied himself a member of law enforcement, sucking up to Buddy whenever he got the chance. "There's a rock with what looks to be blood on it, but we don't know if someone used it as a weapon or if Ms. Whitney somehow slipped and hit her head."

"I'm sure it has to be the latter," Buddy said. "We don't have murders in Eternal Springs. It simply doesn't happen."

While it's true that our island hamlet is hardly a hotbed of gratuitous killing and gang violence, we do experience the occasional murder. Just two months ago, Chet Landry bludgeoned his wife with a frying pan when she refused to help him capture his runaway goats. No, true story. He was appropriately apologetic afterward, but he still maintains it wouldn't have happened if she'd helped him catch the goats. He goes on trial in two weeks. I'm thinking he might get off. Those annoying goats are impossible to wrangle without help, and Sheila always was a lazy loon.

"We can't know exactly what happened yet," Abigail cautioned.

"It was an accident," Buddy stressed.

"We don't know that."

"It was an accident," Buddy persisted, adopting his "I'm the boss" voice. "It couldn't be anything else. This is Eternal

Springs, after all. There's no reason to commit murder in Eternal Springs."

Buddy, always something of a lout, issues edicts and expects everyone to agree with him for no other reason than he's in charge. It often works ... but not with everybody.

"We don't know yet," Abigail shot back, annoyance evident. "I need to get her into my lab and get a better look at her head wound."

"So, what are you waiting for? If I were in charge of this scene I would've gotten her out of here an hour ago. I would've solved things fifty minutes ago. I would've also earned an award for my quick thinking and measured response."

"I found her only forty minutes ago," I pointed out.

"Thank you, Skye." Buddy shot me a quelling look. "You know what I mean. I get things done. Just last week I received an award from the city for being the best mayor in the history of Eternal Springs. Do you know why I got that award?"

"I thought you gave it to yourself."

Kenna elbowed my stomach to quiet me, but I could see the corners of her lips curving and knew that, for once, she didn't want me to keep my mouth shut. She'd been thinking the same thing.

"I did not! The council voted on it."

After he'd put it on the agenda ... and paid for his own plaque. He'd hung it in the middle of city hall. I hear he's considering getting special lights to shine on it so it's impossible for people to miss it. Oh, yeah, that's the other reason everyone in town hates Buddy with a fiery passion. He's the world's biggest braggart and all-around tool. He's just that annoying.

"I think we should focus on the dead woman and not Buddy's well-deserved accolade," Augie interjected, forcing me to mouth the words "suck up" in his direction. "We need to get her inside so Abigail can conduct a proper exam. Right now we don't know if it was intentional or an accident."

"I guarantee it was an accident," Buddy said. "Still, I'm not one for telling others how to do their jobs."

Oh, right. He never does that. Wait ... he always does that.

"If you need to conduct a proper examination, Abigail, I trust you to do it." Buddy turned and lumbered toward his golf cart, Mitzi scampering at his heels. "I trust you all to put this away quickly and quietly. I don't want it dragging out like Chet and that goat thing. Make it go away."

"So much for him having faith in my abilities as the medical examiner," Abigail muttered.

"Just do your job and report your findings," Kenna suggested. "There's nothing else you can do. There's nothing else any of us can do."

That sounded reasonable, but I wasn't feeling reasonable. There were plenty of things I could do. I simply wouldn't tell anyone about them.

Three

I could have left. I wasn't an investigator, after all. It wasn't my job to track down what had happened to Blair Whitney. It was my job to cover her death, though. Well, kind of. No one wanted me to dwell on her death — whether a tragic accident or murder — because it might hurt tourism.

Of course, the needs and wants of others had never informed my decisions. That's how I ended up in this mess in the first place. The incident that shall not be named. No, seriously. I can't talk about it. All that's important is the school burned down and we were stranded here because of our choices that night.

Yeah. I've never been overly fond of consequences.

I watched Abigail work for twenty minutes, my temper growing with each passing second because I was convinced she was incompetent. Augie scattered his men — the finest group of former mall rent-a-cops ever assembled — in various directions to look for evidence. Then he headed my way.

"Are you okay?"

The question caught me off guard. "Compared to what?"

Augie shrugged, discomfort rolling off his shoulders. They were much broader than I'd remembered from high school. That wasn't saying much because he was a science nerd back in school — I know that sounds mean, but he's always irritated me. But he had turned into a relatively handsome man, especially for a guy who would actually take the time to argue with someone over which Death Star design was more flawed.

"I simply want to see if you're okay," Augie explained. "You looked a little pale after ... well, after you tripped over the body."

What exactly was he trying to say? "Pale?"

"Look, it's upsetting." Augie spread his hands out to offer capitulation. We so often went for each other's jugulars that very little thought was spared for the initial assault. He seemed to be signifying that he wasn't in the mood for a fight. That was ... odd.

"I know you pride yourself on being tough and together, but tripping over a dead body would rattle anyone," he continued. "You don't have to be embarrassed by it."

Embarrassed? "Um, I'm not embarrassed."

"You look embarrassed."

"And you look like my feet after a sweaty day of walking," I shot back. Seriously, why does he irritate me so much? It's as if he knows every button to push. "I'm not embarrassed by anything. I'm also not rattled. I don't get rattled."

"Fine." Augie rolled his eyes and raised his hands in defeat. "Excuse me for trying to offer you a shoulder to lean on in your moment of turmoil. I knew it was a mistake when I decided to head over here, but I did it anyway. You don't have to worry about it happening again."

Oh, geez. Drama. He was worse than a teenage girl who lost access to Cosmogirl and her mother's Sephora credit card. I could almost hear him internally crying. "While I'm sure you had good intentions, I am not rattled or embarrassed. You don't have to worry about me."

"Then I won't worry about you."

"Great."

"Good."

We eyed each other for a long beat, the silence serving as a stifling blanket as the heat ratcheted up for the day. Unlike other islands, Eternal Springs didn't suffer through seasons. It had multiple climates to choose from – tropical, winter, lush forest in spring, etc. – and I opted to remain in the hottest locale. That was for several reasons, but the main one was that I needed to be close to the only metropolitan area on the island. I'm one of those people who complain about weather no matter what – I essentially hate being too hot and too cold – so I never lacked for something to grouse about.

Augie, as usual, was the first to break the silence. I thought he'd offer up a pithy goodbye, maybe another stab at my courage upon finding a body, but instead he went the absolute worst route. "Is this some leftover nun thing?"

My mouth dropped open. "Excuse me?"

"St. Joan of Arc. The school you were at until it burned down. You were there to be a nun, right? It would make sense that you were trying to cover your feelings if you were going to become a nun because you believe death is a good thing."

He was simply talking out of his rear end now. He'd always been fascinated by the cover story for the school. St. Joan of Arc, a woman burned at the stake for heresy and later canonized, a woman many people believed was a witch, was supposed to be our patron saint. The name actually made sense, but Augie could only focus on the nun part. He wouldn't let it go.

"I'm not a nun," I reminded him.

"You were going to school to be a nun before everything turned up red and you ended up at school with me," Augie pointed out. "You might not be a nun – and I've often wondered why you just let that go if it was your true calling – but there was a time when you chose that as your path."

Not really. I was never going to be a nun. The town founders were against the idea of the school, even though it was necessary because of the gate that rested underneath it. The original school benefactors had to come up with a cover story, and they went with a convent. I was still furious, even though the decision was made long before I was born.

"How did we even get on this topic?" I let my irritation out to play. "I'm not a nun. I'm not masking my emotions because I was going to be a nun. I'm not upset about tripping over a body. I'm most certainly not embarrassed."

Augie didn't initially react other than to scan my face for a long moment. Then, finally, he heaved out a sigh and ran a hand through his overgrown black hair. "Fine. I'm sorry I asked."

"You should be." I moved to step away from him and then stilled. "Your hair is too long. You need to get it cut."

"I haven't had a chance."

"Well, you should find time." I licked my lips. "As for the other stuff, I know you were simply trying to make me feel better, but it's really not necessary. I'm not suffering because I tripped over a body. It was an accident, simply one of those things that happens."

"I know. But for a second I thought you looked upset."

"Well, I wasn't."

"Good to know."

He'd turned snarky, which meant I had no choice but to react with sarcasm. "Yeah. Thanks for taking a moment to ask about my emotional wellbeing. It means a lot."

Augie made a face. "You're just messing with me now, aren't you?"

I nodded without hesitation. "That's my way."

"Yeah. I'm well aware of that."

I WAITED AT THE SCENE long enough for Augie to become distracted and then I slipped away. There was nothing more that I could do there – not that I was offering much help – and I wanted a chance to glean information about Blair Whitney before Augie realized what I was up to and derailed the information train.

Dylan Potter, a twenty-year-old walking hormone who grew up on the island and developed a weird crush on all the former witches of St. Joan of Arc, stood behind the reception counter, his eyes focused on a computer screen. His presence was a good sign. With all the bigwigs outside he'd have a chance to answer questions without getting in trouble.

This was exactly what I needed.

I pasted a flirty smile on my face as I approached the desk, adding an extra swing to my step as I cleared my throat. Dylan's bland expression turned to overt glee when he realized who was heading his way.

"Hey, Skye." He practically purred when he said my name. "I didn't know you were here today."

"I was out in the lot to cover the ceremony for the addition." I leaned against the counter and offered Dylan a wink. "I wanted to stop in and see you before I left because I was disappointed when I realized you weren't outside. You would've made a long ceremony full of boring speeches tolerable."

Dylan preened under the compliment. He wasn't a bad kid. He was a horn dog of sorts, but all kids that age have the same problem so I didn't take it personally. He wasn't a groper or anything, kept his hands to himself. He was more of a dreamer. Dreams never hurt anyone.

"Oh, that's so sweet." Dylan's smile was so wide it threatened to swallow his entire face, which remained boyish and round. If he ever managed to mature a bit, he'd probably be good looking. It simply hadn't happened for him yet. "Someone had to stay inside and work the desk while everyone else was outside. I'm fifth in line when it comes to being in charge of the reception desk, so it only made sense for me to be the one to remain inside."

"Fifth in line, huh?" I barely managed to swallow a smirk. "How many candidates are in the running for that position?"

"Seven."

"Seven?"

"Well, actually six." Dylan's smile was sweet. "It's seven if you include Janice Thompson, but most people don't include her."

I wrinkled my nose. "Isn't Janice Thompson dead?"

"Yes, but she's still on the employee rolls."

"Oh, well ... hmm." I had no idea what to say to that. It was probably best I move the conversation along. "I need some information about one of your guests."

Dylan's previously amiable expression shifted to something I couldn't quite identify. "You know I'm not supposed to give you information about the guests," he groused. "After the last time ... ."

I cut him off before he could finish. No one needed to be reminded about the last time. I was still suffering from the last time, in fact. I had nightmares. I mean ... who knew that a back waxing sounded like someone was dying? For that matter, who knew that backs could grow that much hair?

"This isn't like last time." I adopted my best "I'm an angel and you can trust me" smile. "That was a tragic accident."

Dylan was stern as he stared me down. "That guy demanded a full refund."

"I didn't mean to scream. I seriously did think that pile of used wax strips was a dead animal."

"He also got comped robes and slippers as an apology," Dylan pointed out.

Ugh. He wasn't going to make it easy. "I swear this time won't be the same as last time." I honestly meant it. "The woman I need information about won't complain about me butting into her business. I can absolutely guarantee that won't happen." Sure, I could only do that because Blair Whitney was dead on the lawn, but Dylan didn't know that.

Dylan heaved a sigh. He wouldn't deny me. He didn't have the strength. "Fine. Who do you need information about?"

"Blair Whitney." I risked a glance over my shoulder to make sure we remained isolated. "I need any information you have on her."

"Blair Whitney?" Dylan furrowed his brow as he typed the name into the computer. He was all business as he scanned the file, although I didn't miss the moment when he stumbled across something of interest ... and that was before he let loose a low whistle.

"What did you find?"

"There're a lot of notes in here about her," Dylan replied. "I mean ... a lot."

"Is that normal?"

"No, and I'm guessing these notes are here so everyone is well aware that she likes things a certain way during her stays."

Hmm. That sounded like code for being difficult. If there were a lot of notes, that most likely meant that Blair made a lot of demands. If she made a lot of demands, that meant she probably complained a lot. If she complained a lot, she probably ticked off a lot of people – both people who worked at the resort and those in her personal life. If she ticked off a lot of people ... you can see where I'm going with this.

"What do the notes say?"

Dylan looked over both shoulders, uncomfortable. "I could get in trouble for this."

"I won't tell a soul."

"That's what you said last time."

"Did I tell anyone you shared information about Mr. Barton with me?"

"No."

"So, what's the problem?"

"The problem is that we were all called into an all-day meeting where we had to learn about being sympathetic and caring to the guests," Dylan answered. "You called him fat and said that the hair probably helped hide the rolls. We all had to pay for that."

I didn't remember saying that. No, really. I've done my best to block that incident from my mind. "Just tell me, Dylan. I promise that what happened last time won't happen again. You can trust me." I batted my eyelashes. "I swear it."

"Fine." Dylan blew out an exaggerated sigh and I swear I heard him mutter something like "come back to bite me" under his breath. He focused on the computer screen, though, and seemed resigned to his fate. "Mrs. Whitney comes here four times a year. She's one of our seasonal sprucers."

I could figure out what that meant. "Yeah. She's had a lot of work done, right?"

"Oh, I can't even go through the entire list of things she's had done. It says one of four pages right at the bottom here. I didn't know we had patient reports that long."

Hmm. "Is she here alone? I mean ... is her husband with her?"

"No. I don't see where her husband has ever visited with her. In fact, some of the notes in her file seem to indicate that something else was going on."

He was being purposely cagey. He knew that drove me crazy. "Just lay it out for me, Dylan. You know you want to."

Dylan looked as if that was the last thing he wanted, but he started talking all the same. "Okay, but you didn't get this from me."

"Of course not."

"Mrs. Whitney is here with her daughter, her daughter's best friend, the friend's mother and some sort of personal assistant."

I had no idea why Dylan seemed to think that was important information. "And?"

"And there's a note in here to make sure that Mrs. Whitney and the best friend are never left alone together."

"And why is that?"

"Because apparently the best friend is having sex with Mrs. Whitney's husband."

I couldn't hide my shock. "Seriously?"

Dylan nodded, solemn. "There's a big notation in here. I mean ... there's like two pages of warnings and explanations about how everybody knows one another."

That was too much information to coax Dylan into reading aloud. "I don't suppose you'd print that for me, would you?"

Dylan balked. "That's going too far."

It was. I didn't feel good about putting him in this position. I might need to refer back to the notes, though, and I couldn't risk walking away without them. Once word spread that Blair Whitney was dead there was no chance I'd get a gander at those notes. "It's really important."

"But ... I could lose my job."

I took pity on him. "I'll dance with you at karaoke this week if you print those records for me."

Dylan was caught. We both knew it. "Oh, well ... ."

"It can be a slow song."

Dylan must have realized he had negotiating power because he took control of the situation. "Will you wear a short dress?"

Ugh. "Sure."

"Something blue to match your eyes."

"Yes."

"That tie-dye dress with the low-cut top."

Hmm. Exactly how much attention had he been paying to my wardrobe? "I'll wear the dress, Dylan. I'll even let you pick the song that we dance to."

Dylan beamed and I thought he was done with his demands. I wasn't that lucky. "And no bra!"

Good grief. "Don't push your luck." I narrowed my eyes and extended a finger. "I'll hurt you if you ever demand that again."

Dylan's expression turned sheepish. "I never know when to stop from going too far."

That was a trait we shared. "Just print what you've got. I promise to make the rest of it happen on Friday. You have my word."

Dylan was back to being happy as he extended his hand for me to shake. "It's been a pleasure doing business with you."

Yeah, yeah, yeah.

Four

I ran into Augie when I was leaving. In my haste to stuff the records into my messenger bag – a must when driving a Vespa – I had my head down and didn't notice him until I was already crashing into his solid chest.

"Whoa!" Augie grabbed my arms to keep me from tumbling as I bounced back. "Where's the fire?"

Crappity crap crap crap! "Nowhere." I shoved the printed sheets into the bag and adopted an innocent expression. "I was simply looking down and didn't see you."

"Uh-huh." Augie didn't look convinced. "Why are you in here?"

Good question. It deserved a good lie. Thankfully I was good at thinking them up on the fly. "I needed a bottle of water because I was feeling a little shaky. I didn't want to bother anyone inside so I grabbed one from Dylan."

Augie leaned to the right slightly so he could look over my shoulder. I resisted the urge to follow his gaze because I feared the increased attention would be enough to make Dylan crack. I fully expected him to crack, of course, but as long as it happened after I was safely away I was fine with it.

Unlike me, Dylan didn't do well under pressure, and he was the absolute worst when it came to thinking up lies.

"Water, huh?" Augie made a loud throat-clearing sound to get Dylan's attention. "Hey, Dylan, do you know why Ms. Thornton was here today?"

Well, great. Augie always was the suspicious sort, even when I manufactured a perfectly good lie that almost anyone else would believe. "I just told you."

"I want to hear what Dylan has to say." Augie's expression told me he was determined to figure out exactly what I was up to. That wouldn't bode well for me. I needed to distract him for thirty seconds, just long enough for me to slip out the door and get to my Vespa.

"Dylan is a busy boy," I argued, taking a careful step to the left to increase the distance between Augie and me. "He doesn't need you harassing him."

"I'm not harassing him." Augie's full attention was on Dylan, which allowed me to take another four steps. I was almost through the door. I was going to make it. "I simply want to know what Ms. Thornton was doing here, Dylan. It's an easy question."

I flicked my eyes to Dylan and found his face red with effort as he struggled to come up with something to say. He really was a moron sometimes. I couldn't believe I had to dance with him Friday ... and I was sure he would pick some monstrous power ballad that would make me want to retch. That was the kid's way. Still, a deal was a deal.

"She was ... looking for something to drink," Dylan supplied.

For one brief moment I thought the kid was going to come through for me. I couldn't believe it. He came up with a lie and it was the same one I'd already told. What were the odds?

"She wanted whiskey, but I told her we didn't have any,"

Dylan continued. "She should know better because we're a health spa, and I'm not allowed to serve drinks because I'm not twenty-one yet."

And then it all came crashing down. Son of a ... !

"Whiskey, Skye?" Augie turned as I bolted out the door and scurried toward the parking lot. I heard Augie scrambling after me, but I refused to turn around. "Skye!" He sounded furious.

I offered up a half-hearted wave over my shoulder but kept my eyes on my Vespa, keys already in hand. "It was great seeing you, Augie. I'm sure we'll meet up again."

"You can count on it."

I DIDN'T BREATHE EASY until I was back in town and free of Augie's evil determination. I had no doubt he'd find me later – curiosity was often to blame for killing more than cats and Augie was blessed with an overabundance of it – but that was a problem for future Skye to tackle. Present Skye only cared about getting some green tea and going through the notes Dylan supplied.

I headed for the closest coffee shop. Despite its size, Eternal Springs has more than one to keep the tourists happy. I was an everyday customer at this one. It was still early, so the shop was mostly empty. Except for Zola Meadows, the owner of Cackleberries plant shop, who sat at a central table with her auburn hair pulled back in a simple ponytail.

"Hey." I dropped my stack of papers on the table and signaled the girl behind the counter for my drink of choice. "What are you doing here?"

"I thought I'd try to solve the problem of world peace," Zola replied dryly, rolling her eyes as she gestured toward what looked to be a glass of passion fruit tea over ice. "It's going splendidly."

I didn't bother to hide my sour attitude. "Well, at least you have goals for the day." I exhaled heavily as I took the chair next to her and wrinkled my forehead when I realized she was thumbing through a plant catalog. "What's new for the upcoming season? I think you'd look fabulous in lavender."

"Your wit always manages to brighten my day. Have I ever told you that?"

"No." I dug in my pocket for cash and handed it to the barista when she delivered my drink, waiting for her to leave before continuing. "Something tells me that you're not really a big fan of my wit."

"What was your first clue?"

"I think the scowl when you saw it was me walking through the door was a giveaway."

"Well, at least I have that going for me." Zola's tone was cool as she sipped her tea and flipped through the catalog. "Is there a reason you're here bugging me rather than working in the middle of the day?"

"Is there a reason you're being such a soggy tampon?"

"Ugh." Zola made a disgusted sound in the back of her throat. She was much more prim and proper than the rest of our group. Oh, yeah, right. She's a St. Joan of Arc survivor, too. That makes her a witch, the same as Kenna and me. While my talents rested in the air and Kenna's burned hot with fire, Zola was an earth witch. She wasn't as flashy with her magic, something she never tired of reminding us about. "Must you be so crude?"

I shrugged, unbothered by her tone. "I believe it's genetic. I didn't have a choice in the matter."

"You had a choice." Zola ran her tongue over her teeth as she took a moment to give me a long once-over. "Why are you all sweaty?"

"Maybe I'm hot and bothered for you."

"Or maybe you're up to something." Zola knew me too well. Sometimes I could feel her eyes tearing through me, as if searching for answers that she could magically rip from my soul. It wasn't a comfortable feeling. She knew that, of course, and used it to her advantage. "You are up to something. Where were you this morning?"

She's also the "mom" of the group. It has something to do with being in touch with her earthy roots. It's beyond annoying. "Why do you care?"

"You're acting odd — even odder than usual, which is a terrifying thought — and I want to know what to expect when trouble catches up with you." Zola was matter-of-fact. "Where were you this morning? Wait, I already know. You were at the resort. They had the dedication of the new building this morning. They were teasing it on the radio station."

Of course they were. Eternal Springs was so small that the island's main source of entertainment — a radio station that was stuck in the eighties — covered every lame event that happened at the resort. It was grating.

"I was there."

Zola narrowed her eyes. "Why are you here then? Those things usually go for two or three hours."

"This one never really went at all." I saw no reason to lie. "I tripped over a dead body and that derailed the whole thing."

Zola finally showed real interest in the conversation as her eyes lit with keen intrigue. "You tripped over a body? How?"

"Well, you know how I'm always so graceful and watch where I'm going? I was doing that this morning when I decided to cut across the lawn because I wanted to make sure I was in my seat before anyone started speaking."

"That's because Kenna was there and you didn't want her to singe your tail."

She wasn't wrong. "Are you going to listen to the story or keep interrupting?"

"Fine. I'm listening."

"Anyway, I was cutting across the lawn when I tripped," I explained. "I didn't realize there was a body under me until I was already sprawled on top of her."

"That's a lovely visual."

"Someone bashed her head in with a rock," I added.

Zola shifted in her chair, mirth turning to worry. "She was murdered?"

"That's my take on the situation. Buddy feels differently."

"Buddy? What does Buddy have to do with anything?" Zola's expression reflected what everyone in town felt when Buddy's name came up. The guy was a pimple on the butt of humanity. No one liked him. I even had my doubts that his wife liked him.

"He was called out when we found the body," I replied. "He left the investigation in Abigail and Augie's hands, which means they're going to do five minutes of work and declare it an accident. I know better."

Zola didn't look convinced as she sipped from her straw. "And how do you know better?"

"She was in a weird spot to trip and fall on a rock." I'd been picturing the scene for the better part of an hour and I already had a hunch. "It was flat. The rock was one of those ornate ones they use to line the flowerbeds to make them look cutesy or whatever you call rock accents near bushes."

Zola snorted. "Your landscaping knowledge truly is a wonder." She chewed her bottom lip as she turned to look at the front door when the overhead bell jangled. I could see who was entering – and I had no interest in Carol Kennedy and her screaming twins of terror – so I took advantage of Zola's momentary distraction to yank the straw from her drink, lick it and then shove it back in place. "Ugh. I hate the

Kennedy twins. I swear they're going to grow up to be sociopathic serial killers."

She wasn't the only one who had considered that possibility. "They're three. They won't be committing murders for at least a decade. I want to focus on this murder." I pulled the sheets of paper Dylan supplied from my bag and smoothed them. "It seems the dead woman was on vacation with her daughter and three other women when the attack happened."

"Alleged attack," Zola corrected. "You don't know that she was really attacked."

"I have a feeling."

"Last month you had a feeling that someone was watching you from the woods outside your house," Zola pointed out. "You said you thought it was a vampire."

Of course she'd bring that up. "It could've been a vampire."

"Sure. Stranger things have happened in Eternal Springs. But it wasn't a vampire, was it?"

"No." I made a face. "It was that horrible hairless cat that runs around judging me."

"I believe his name is Tut. He's a sphinx."

"I think his name is Satan and he wants to drive me insane." The hairless cat was one of a posse that wandered Eternal Springs doing whatever they wanted. The former familiars of our witchy sisters refused to move on when the school burned down. They wouldn't leave and now they were breeding like ... well, like cats in heat. The business folk didn't really mind them – they made for great stories to share with tourists and kept the vermin population in check – but I minded them. They were monstrous little busybodies and know-it-alls. Especially Tut the Terrible. He liked to agitate me most. It was almost as if he knew that a hairless cat was the stuff of my nightmares.

"His name is Tut and he only bothers you because you

allow him to." Zola was pragmatic as she grabbed one of the sheets of paper from my stack. "What is this?"

"I sweet talked Dylan into printing the dead woman's file. Apparently she was a regular. They had a bunch of notes jotted down about her because she was difficult."

"So I see." Zola didn't bother to hide her surprise as she read. "It says here she was on vacation with her husband's mistress. That can't be normal."

"That's what I said."

"You said she was with her daughter and three other women. You failed to mention that one of those women was openly known to be her husband's ... um ... friend."

"Ugh. You're such a prude." I snatched back the sheet of paper. "That's one of the other reasons I think it had to be murder. I mean, you just don't go on vacation with your husband's harlot and play nice. I'm sure words were exchanged and things got out of hand."

"So you think it was the mistress."

I shrugged. "Who else?"

"Well, I hate to encourage you because everyone knows you've got an out-of-control imagination, but I've seen the woman in that photo before ... and recently." Zola looked a little too smug for comfort. "I bet you didn't know that."

I was in no mood for games. "You saw this woman in town recently?"

Zola nodded. "She was with someone we all know and ... well, love certainly isn't the word ... but we all know him."

Oh, well, now things were getting interesting. "Who?"

Zola lowered her voice to a conspiratorial whisper. "Guess."

I freaking hate games. "Just tell me!"

"Guess."

"Tell me or I'll send Swoops over to poop in your plants," I threatened.

Zola's previously smug smile tipped down into a pronounced frown. "You need to stop telling him to do that. He's ruining my fuchsias."

I feigned innocence. "I thought I read somewhere that bat droppings are good for plant growth."

"He drops enough to choke the life out of the plants and you know it. What are you feeding him, by the way? I don't think his dietary needs are being met."

"He eats anything and everything. He's on the hunt for corned beef hash today, so if you have any in your house hide it. He's not above breaking and entering."

"Ugh. Who would eat corned beef hash? It looks like somebody already ate it. No wonder my fuchsias are dying."

Zola is supposed to be the easygoing one of our group, but she often lapses into bouts of whining that make me want to deafen myself with Q-tips ... or at least gag her with a chloroform-soaked rag. What? She wouldn't die from it. Sometimes she simply makes me want to take a nap.

"Listen, as entertaining as I find this conversation, I really need to focus on Blair Whitney," I prodded, turning back to business. "Who did you see her with?"

"Oh, right." Zola shook her head, perhaps dislodging thoughts of Swoops and his magical powers of fertilization. "She was with Buddy."

I stiffened, the words taking me by surprise. "Buddy? Our Buddy?"

"Do you know anyone else who would willingly coin his own nickname and then insist everyone in town use it?"

"That can't be right." I shook my head as the possibility washed over me. "Buddy was there. I told you he was there. He saw Blair Whitney's body. He didn't act as if he knew her."

"Huh." Zola tapped her bottom lip, thoughtful. "Are you sure he saw her? I mean ... maybe he didn't look very closely.

Not everyone wants to get up close and personal with a dead woman."

"I guess that's possible." I shook my head. "I swear he looked at her. I think he knew who she was. Do you know what ties they had to each other?"

"I don't. I only know they were seen having lunch together at the diner. A few people were gossiping because poor Mitzi was nowhere to be found while Buddy and this woman spent a very long meal together. The word being bandied about regarding their interaction was 'intimate.'"

And things simply got more intriguing the more I learned. "Thanks." I was distracted when I got to my feet and shoved the records back in my bag. "You've been a great help."

"I aim to please." Zola beamed as she lifted the straw from her drink and sucked from the bottom end, clearly enjoying her position as gossip queen of the world.

"I licked your straw when you weren't looking," I added. What? It's only fair to share things like that.

"Ugh!" Zola tossed the straw down on the table. "Why do you do that?"

Ah, a question for the ages. "I'll talk to you later. I have some things to check out."

Five

I could have tracked down Buddy and asked him directly, but that wasn't really my style. I was sneakier than that. Besides, Buddy was a pain in the keister, but he was smart enough to evade me. His wife was a different story.

I didn't know much about Mitzi Montgomery and what I did know didn't make me like her. In fact, most everything I knew about the woman steered me toward strong dislike. Despite that, I felt sorry for her.

She was a gossipy girl who'd hung with her clique in high school, never breaking out and trying to get to know anyone else. That went for my witchy sisters and me as much as anybody else. When we were suddenly thrust into public school after attending what everyone assumed was a convent the welcome wasn't exactly warm.

Of course, the other students were mildly frightened of us because of our "close personal relationship with God" – that was something Zola thought up to use as a weapon should we be attacked by catty teenagers – so the students weren't exactly mean because they didn't want to get on God's bad side (you know, just in case). But they weren't what I would call welcoming either.

Mitzi ran with a different crew back then. Buddy was almost twenty years older and didn't deign to hang with the youngsters. They didn't hook up until two years after graduation, and by then some of the shine had left Mitzi. She was no longer queen of the high school, whatever she thought would happen to propel her to queen of the world status suddenly forgotten.

Mitzi and Buddy's initial dating raised plenty of eyebrows and sparked untold whispering and speculation. What would someone like Mitzi want with someone like Buddy? In truth, Buddy wasn't all bad. He was a braggart of the worst degree, turning every conversation to himself rather than listening to others. He lost interest in any conversation that didn't revolve around him. He delegated authority with a cool hand, making his Eternal Springs underlings do all the heavy lifting when a situation couldn't be turned to garner publicity for Buddy himself. That's when he lost interest, you see. The moment he realized he couldn't gain attention or talk about himself, he wanted to move on to something else.

That's why his hookup with Mitzi didn't go unnoticed. She believed the world revolved around her in high school, so it seemed they wouldn't be a good fit. They surprised everyone when they not only survived dating but opted to marry. They'd been going strong for a decade, although they hadn't added any little Montgomery babies to their happy home. I harbored a strong suspicion that Mitzi became fixated on knitting so she could channel her aggression into something other than strangling Buddy when he began talking about himself.

Mitzi became something of a tight-lipped loner since the marriage, spending all her time being Buddy's wife rather than her own person. Everything she did was for him ... or about him ... or because of him. She was no longer a force unto her own. She was the person who dedicated herself to making Buddy's life easier.

There was one little spot where Mitzi continued to shine, and that was her thrice-weekly radio show. As I mentioned before, the radio station is one of the few sources of entertainment in Eternal Springs since internet is spotty, which makes streaming services a waste of money (and network television is all kinds of terrible now). That means we have a lot of talk radio and craft shows to get people through the day. One of those craft shows is "Knitter's Circle with Mitzi Montgomery." It's so boring people often add an extra word after "circle" – you can figure it out if you have a filthy mind – and there's talk that the show should be bottled and sold as a cure for insomnia.

People are mean. What can I say? Fine. I started the insomnia cure joke. It's totally true, though.

I let myself into the HEX 66.6 building without knocking or waiting for someone to grant me entrance, instead muttering a small spell that caused the lock to tumble and door to spring open. There were only two cameras watching the perimeter and they were both located in Evian Brooks' office. In addition to being the owner of the radio station, she was the fourth witch in our little cursed square. She's the water witch ... and she's just as much of a pain as the other two. In fact, I'm the only one who is a true delight. The others are stereotypical ... well, witches.

Evian didn't seem surprised to see me when I popped into her office. I threw open the door and made my presence known with a flourish – actually, I let loose a bit of my air magic and allowed it to blow back Evian's hair (something I knew she absolutely hated) – and then strolled to one of the uncomfortable chairs on the other side of her desk and sank into it.

"You always did love a good entrance," Evian complained, smoothing her brown hair.

"I missed my calling," I agreed, making a big show of studying my stubby fingernails. "I should've been an actress. Instead I got stuck here ... seemingly forever."

"And whose fault is that?"

I dragged my eyes to her face. "If you say mine, things are going to go from soap opera dramatic to WWE dramatic."

Evian rolled her eyes. "Whatever. Why are you even here? You rarely stop by for a visit in the middle of the week. Heck, you don't on weekends either. I think I can count on one hand the number of times you've been inside this building for something other than a mandated story."

"I've visited plenty of times." Most of them when Evian wasn't expecting me, so she didn't know. "As for why I'm here today, I need to talk with the talent as soon as she's done inducing everyone to afternoon naps."

It took Evian a moment to grasp what I was saying. "You want to talk to Mitzi."

"That's what I said."

"But ... why?"

"Maybe I'm looking to widen my circle of friends. Have you ever considered that?"

"Not even a little."

Yeah, I should've come up with a convincing lie before visiting. That would've been the smart thing to do. "I need to talk to her about Buddy."

Evian made a face. "Why would anyone want to talk about Buddy? He does it enough for all of us."

"Yes, but he was seen having lunch yesterday with a woman who turned up dead and I want to figure out how he knew her and why he was chatting her up."

Evian absently scratched her cheek. "I think I'm behind. What dead woman?"

I told her about Blair Whitney's unfortunate demise. "Zola said Buddy was having lunch with the victim at the diner yesterday. He didn't even act like he recognized her when he saw her body at the resort. There has to be a reason for that."

"Have you considered that he simply didn't look too closely at the body?" Evian challenged. "I don't know about anyone else, but I'd make it a point to look anywhere but at a dead person if I had the choice."

"That's because you're a wimp."

"Or human," Evian corrected. "Still, you don't know that she was murdered. It could've been an accident."

It could have been an accident. But I knew deep down it wasn't. "I just want to talk to Mitzi. I figure she'll know about her husband's relationship with the plastic surgery addict."

"You don't know she was a plastic surgery addict."

"I've seen her records. They go on for four pages. She's had more nips and tucks than the cast of *The Golden Girls* during their heyday."

"Nice." Evian rolled her eyes. "Have you considered that Mitzi won't know about Buddy's relationship with Blair Whitney? I mean ... if he was doing it on the sly he purposely cut her out of the loop."

I had considered that ... and then immediately dismissed the idea. "Mitzi always knows where Buddy is and what he is doing. Even if he didn't tell her who he was having lunch with, she knew."

Evian tilted her head to the side, considering, and finally sighed. "You're probably right. Just wait until Mitzi is done with her show. Most people wouldn't notice if you questioned her live, but she does have one or two fans."

I had my doubts, but it was only twenty minutes. I could wait her out. "Great. I ... ." I frowned when I got to my feet and recognized the water mark on the crotch of my khaki capris. I hadn't even felt it spreading. She was that good. "You did that on purpose."

Evian's smile was enigmatic. "I have no idea what you're talking about."

"Yeah, yeah." I stomped toward the hallway, ideas of drying myself under the powerful hand units in the bathroom dancing through my head. "I'll pay you back for this," I warned.

"I expect nothing less."

"MITZI, DO YOU have a moment?"

Mitzi jolted when I practically pounced on her as she left the recording booth. Her eyes momentarily widened, reminding me of a trapped animal, until she recovered and regained her senses.

"You gave me a fright, Skye." She pressed her hand to the spot above her heart. "You should make a noise before scaring the life out of someone. That's simply proper etiquette."

Of course she would go *there*. "I'm sorry." I didn't mean it, not even a little. "I thought you saw me as you were walking out. I didn't mean to frighten you."

"Yes, well, I guess it doesn't matter." Mitzi has an annoying habit of forcing an extremely chipper and upbeat attitude. I absolutely hate it. It's unbelievably fake. I'd much prefer dealing with the same petulant teenager I knew way back when because at least that persona felt real. This one was ... well, something else entirely. "Did you need something?"

The question dragged me back to reality. "I have a few questions for you."

"For me?" Mitzi didn't bother to hide her surprise. "Why would you want to talk to me?"

"Maybe I find you interesting."

BAT OUT OF SPELL

Mitzi didn't as much as blink as she pinned me with a dark look. Yeah, I should've known she wouldn't fall for that.

"Maybe I need to track down information about the dead woman at the spa and I found out Buddy had ties to her," I stared right back. There really was no reason to lie to her. "Her name is Blair Whitney, and my understanding is that she was with Buddy yesterday."

Mitzi was good at hiding her emotions – she'd spent years pretending Buddy wasn't the most annoying man on the planet, after all – but I didn't miss the hint of panic that flitted through her eyes. She was terrified about ... something.

"I have no idea who Blair Whitney is," Mitzi offered, recovering quickly. "That name doesn't mean anything to me."

She was lying. She wasn't terrible at it, but she was nowhere near as good at it as me. She was very definitely lying. The question was why?

"So the people who saw Buddy lunching with Blair at the diner yesterday were lying?" I challenged. "My bad. I'll just head down there and see if I can get a copy of the security camera footage. I know they keep it for a few days. That should clear things right up."

"Wait!" Mitzi desperately lashed out and grabbed my arm, tightening her grip on my elbow until her fingernails dug in and caused me to want to yelp. I managed to refrain, but just barely. I'm a baby when I want to be. "You can't go talking out of turn about Buddy and Blair."

Ha! They did know each other. "Let's take it from the top," I suggested, delicately extricating my arm from Mitzi's talon-like grip. "You really should think about letting go of the acrylic nails. Maybe try some gels or something. I'm sure they'll hurt less than ... that."

Mitzi wasn't even remotely apologetic. "What do you

want, Skye? We both know you're not here to ask innocent questions. You think you know something."

That was interesting. Mitzi's bitterness was so pronounced that common sense had yet to prevail. There was no way I could know the truth because it had been only two hours since I'd discovered the body. Even I didn't move that fast.

"I want to know about Buddy's relationship with Blair," I said. "Why were they having lunch together yesterday?"

"Perhaps you should ask him."

"I'm asking you," I shot back. "Either tell me or I will go straight to him. I'm guessing that will put him in a bad mood when I tell him you could've fixed everything by answering my questions. That's just a guess, of course."

Mitzi narrowed her eyes to dangerous slits. "You wouldn't dare."

"You'd be surprised what I'd do." I'd gone this far so there was no backing down now. "I want to know what Buddy was doing with Blair Whitney. If you don't tell me, I'll be forced to come up with my own conclusions ... and you know how my mind works."

Mitzi was appropriately disgusted. "Yes. Sewers are cleaner."

I snorted. "Good one. Now tell me about Buddy and Blair."

Mitzi turned somber, her shoulders drooping as she wrung her hands. "I don't know what to tell you. The lunch wasn't a big deal. It's not as if Buddy was cheating on me or anything. Don't even think about spreading that rumor."

Given his size, I often wondered how Buddy managed to keep his wife satisfied. That was another reason I thought she immersed herself in her knitting. I wisely decided to keep that to myself for the time being. "I don't think Buddy was cheating on you." That was mostly true. "I know he had lunch with a woman who turned up dead, though, and then he pretended he didn't recognize her. There has to be a reason for that."

Mitzi balked. "He was surprised. I mean ... stunned really. He didn't believe his own eyes at the time. He wasn't trying to be purposely evasive."

She sounded convincing and yet I wasn't sure I believed her. "What is Blair Whitney to Buddy?"

"She's ... um ... an old friend."

Yeah, and that sounded even less convincing. "Fine." I threw up my hands in feigned defeat. "I'll take my questions to Buddy. I don't have time to play games with you."

"Don't you even think about it!" Mitzi practically screeched the words as she clawed at my arm. "He's having a rough enough time now without having to deal with you."

I had no idea what to make of that statement. "Let's try this again, Mitzi," I gritted out through clenched teeth. "Tell me how Buddy and Blair knew each other – and do it right now – or I will track down your husband and start peppering him with uncomfortable questions. Those are your only two options."

Mitzi's glare told me whatever animosity she harbored would be doubled after this altercation, but I couldn't be troubled to care.

"Fine." Mitzi blew out a frustrated sigh that caused her dark bangs to flutter. "Buddy and Blair went to college together. It was a lifetime ago and it wasn't a big deal."

There were hints of truth in Mitzi's response, but that didn't explain everything. "Why hide it?"

"Blair didn't want anyone to know she went to a community college – especially in New Jersey, although I have no idea why that would be such a big deal. And she wanted to keep the meeting on the down low."

"So, she's not from around here?"

Mitzi shook her head. "The mainland."

"And she's just an old friend of Buddy's?"

Mitzi enthusiastically bobbed her head, as if she were trying to convince me with chin movements alone. "They've known each other a long time. It's completely innocent. Buddy is not to blame for this. He has no motive, and you know what a good guy he is."

Oh, I knew. He told everyone he ran across what a good guy he was. He wanted to make sure people understood the magnitude of his greatness. "Are you sure that's it, Mitzi?" I wanted to believe her – part of me did, in fact – but something still felt off. I couldn't put a name to it.

"I'm sure." Mitzi folded her arms across her chest. "It's simply a terrible coincidence."

There were a lot of terrible things going on in regard to Blair Whitney. I didn't think any of them were coincidences.

"Well, thanks for your time." I pasted a bright smile on my face. "I'll let you get back to your knitting."

"So, you'll let it go?" Mitzi looked hopeful.

"Of course," I lied. "Buddy is a good guy. He'd never do anything to hurt anyone."

Mitzi needed to hear them, so I said the words. That didn't mean I believed them, at least entirely. There was definitely something else going on here.

Six

I went home after leaving the radio station. I needed to think and I wasn't a fan of doing that in public places.

Swoops had clearly been on a rampage during my absence. Every bra and panty set I owned was strewn about the living room. I narrowed my eyes when I realized he'd actually taken the time to make the lamp look like a busty woman. I screeched at the second floor, where I knew he was hiding.

"Why do you feel the need to do this?"

Swoops didn't immediately answer. In fact, it was so quiet I wondered if he'd fled outside to avoid my wrath. Then I realized I was only kidding myself. Swoops would never deny himself the joy he received when watching me melt down, so I studied the spindles at the top of the stairs for a hint of movement.

"Come down here and pick up your mess," I ordered, adopting my best school master voice. "I didn't make this mess and I want you to pick it up."

Still nothing. I would have to try something else. "I brought you a present." I dug in my messenger bag until I came up with two cans of corned beef hash. I made one brief stop on my way home because I figured bribery might be in order depending on the plan I came up with, so I was prepared for Swoops' special brand of Armageddon.

Corned beef hash. Corned beef hash.

He hooted and chirped as he suddenly appeared on the landing that led to the second floor.

I cocked an eyebrow. "Yes. It's your favorite."

Yum. Feed now.

I shook my head. "You have to clean up the mess you made if you expect me to cook this for you." I adopted a stern expression. "You know the rules. If you make a mess, you have to clean it up."

I didn't make a mess.

I offered an incredulous expression as I widened my arms and gestured toward the explosion of panties and bras. "Well, I certainly didn't make this mess."

Not me. Not me. More tittering as his belligerence ratcheted up a notch.

"Really?" I so wasn't in the mood for my theatrical familiar and his unique brand of mayhem. "If you didn't do it, who did?"

Clover did it. Not me. Never me.

I wrinkled my forehead. Clover? It wasn't out of the realm of possibility. Clover was Zola's familiar, a cute little skunk who acted like a lovable dog when strangers got a gander at her. She loved being petted and pretended to be roadkill so people would stop and then exclaim in delight when she made a miraculous recovery. Yeah, I found it a bit cloying, too.

"Clover did this?" I prowled through the house for an entry point. I'd spent the better part of two weeks familiar-proofing my house because that hairless cat beast kept getting inside and spouting fortune cookie nonsense while sitting on my chest and making me believe I was suffocating as I jerked out of a dream every morning. "How did she get in?"

Hole.

"What hole?"

Kitchen door.

There was a hole in the kitchen door? I was going to go scorched earth on that skunk if that was true.

I stalked into the kitchen and planted the cans of corned beef hash on the counter, ignoring Swoops as he fluttered into the room and landed next to them. He made cooing sounds as I studied the bottom of the aluminum door, frowning when I realized something had indeed knocked out the center panel to gain entrance.

"Son of a ... ! I'm going to turn that skunk into real roadkill if she's not careful."

Cook. Cook. Cook.

I cast an irritated glance over my shoulder and found Swoops rubbing himself over the cans. It was almost as if he were caught in a romantic dance of sorts. "Clean up the living room and I'll cook it for you."

Now.

"Clean first."

Cook first.

"I will cook when you're finished cleaning," I snapped. "I pay the bills here. That means I'm in charge."

Swoops narrowed his onyx eyes. *Cook.*

"Clean."

Ugh. Swoops staggered across the counter and clutched his wings to his chest as he mimed a fainting spell. *Feeling weak. I will surely die without food.*

"You're not going to die."

Fading away. Fast. He fell to the counter and fanned a wing.

The light is fading. I'm coming to the other side, Mama. I will be with you soon.

Since Swoops' late mother was my former familiar, a surly creature who liked to hide in the toilet and bite when I got up to use the facilities in the middle of the night, I had trouble mustering any sympathy. "If you see your mother tell her I don't miss her."

Mama. I'm crossing into the light. I don't want to be alone when it happens. I hope you're waiting for me so I don't cross the Rainbow Bridge by myself.

"Oh, geez." I pinched the bridge of my nose. "If I cook the hash, do you promise to pick up that mess you let the skunk make while you were supposed to be guarding the house?"

Swoops opened one eye. *Yes. But hurry. My life force is draining.*

"Your life force is fine," I muttered, grabbing a skillet from the cabinet beneath the counter and glaring. "I can't believe I fall for this every single time."

Cook. I can feel the life flowing into me again. But it might only be temporary.

"Yeah, yeah, yeah."

SWOOPS DID NOT CLEAN the living room. I really didn't expect him to. In addition to being overly dramatic he is ridiculously lazy. Once he finished his corned beef hash – all the time eyeing me because I made some for myself – he declared he needed a nap and disappeared to the hammock I'd installed for him in the corner of the living room. There he proceeded to snore so loudly I couldn't come up with a good idea on how next to approach my project.

That's how I ended up in the woods by the resort. I needed cackleberries, and they were available in only one spot ... which just happened to be near the Cottonmouth Copse. No, that's not its real name. I call it that because the trees there are the sarcastic sort because they drink from the Blathering Brook and essentially spend their days drunk.

No, you didn't mishear me. In this particular spot the trees are alive with something other than the sound of music.

"Well, look who it is. It's Little Miss I Swear Like a Trucker."

I cringed at Agatha's voice. She was only one of the trees in the copse, but she almost always insisted on talking first. For the record, not everyone can hear the trees. It's a witch ability (one I wish I didn't have) and the trees get overly chatty when we pay them visits because they spend a lot of time isolated and watching the doings in Eternal Springs from afar. They like having something other than fellow trees to poke.

"Good afternoon, ladies and gentlemen," I trilled, doing my best to pretend I was happy to partake in the visit. "How is everyone doing this fine and wondrous day?"

"Oh, she's been smoking the wacky-tobaccy again," one of the other female trees said. I couldn't quite identify her voice because she often got fed up and ignored me when I visited. "That can be the only explanation."

"I haven't been smoking wacky-tobaccy," I shot back dryly. "If I had, you can bet I wouldn't waste the buzz visiting you guys."

"You're always so grumpy when you visit," one voice said. "Why are you so unhappy?"

"Yes, Skye, why are you so unhappy?" Agatha intoned. "Why are you so profoundly whiny? Why do you insist on swearing rather than choosing your words? Why can't you be pleasant for five minutes of every day?"

Ugh. I so did not come out here for this abuse. "I need

cackleberries. I promise I won't hang around long, so there's no reason to get your leaves in a bunch."

"Such a funny girl," Agatha said. "I can't believe you're still single with a mouth like that."

In Agatha's world, almost everything I said was akin to a curse word. She didn't think I carried myself like a proper lady. I was totally fine with that. I didn't want to be a proper lady. That was the one thing I never wanted. Because her soul was left over from another time – she helped run the school at its inception – she looked at things in a very different manner.

"I can't either." I was blasé as I shuffled past the trees, taking a moment to gesture toward the sky and give Swoops a pointed look. "I made you corned beef hash. You need to take to the skies and make sure someone doesn't sneak up on me while I'm collecting berries and insults."

Swoops made a dramatic face. *I should be taking a nap.*

"And I should be anywhere but where I am," I shot back. "Get off your duff and take to the sky. I don't want to get caught out here talking to a bunch of trees ... and you."

Whatever. Swoops did as instructed, although I didn't miss the disdainful look he lobbed in my direction before taking flight. He'd find a way to pay me back for bossing him around. He always did.

Once he was airborne, I got to work collecting the cackleberries. I got the idea to use them when I couldn't get over the fact that Mitzi appeared to be lying even while purporting to tell the truth. I had no doubt that Buddy and Blair went to college together. That would be stupid for her to lie about and it could easily be verified. Even if I had to place a call to the home office to get it done thanks to our spotty internet, I could most definitely find the information. So she wasn't lying about that.

She was lying about something, though. I simply had to figure out what. The only foolproof way I knew to outsmart liars was to force them to tell the truth. And how do you do that? Truth serum, of course. Unfortunately for me, the crop of cackleberries was weak this year, so I needed almost everything on the bushes to make a full batch. I couldn't risk making a half batch in case I needed doses for other people ... including the mistress who just happened to go on vacation with my victim. I still couldn't figure out why anyone would think that was a good idea. I might need truth serum for the lot before I was done.

"There were big goings on at the resort today," Earl announced. He was the one tree that didn't make me want to grab a chainsaw. He kept the sarcasm to a minimum and was always amiable.

"Yeah. A woman died." I began stripping berries and adding them to the small container I'd brought. "She was bashed over the head with a rock."

"Really?" Agatha made a tutting sound. "Things like that didn't happen in my day."

"They did, but it was simply easier to fudge evidence back then," I countered. "Her death hasn't technically been ruled a homicide, but I know she was murdered. There's no way that was an accident."

"Well, if you know better than law enforcement you must be in the right," Agatha drawled.

Ugh. Seriously. Why didn't I think to bring matches ... or a box of those emerald ash borer bugs? That would shut her up. "I'm just saying that it's very unlikely that woman died by accidental means. Someone wanted her dead ... and now she's dead."

"That's an interesting theory."

I froze when I heard the new voice, swiveling slowly so I could focus on the individual who had managed to sneak up when I wasn't looking. So much for my bat spy in the sky. I was so going to make him pay.

"Hello, Augie." I did my best to appear as if kneeling in the woods while plucking berries and talking to trees he couldn't hear was the most normal thing in the world. "Fancy meeting you here."

"Yes, it is fancy," Augie agreed, his expression dark as he scanned the small clearing. "Can I ask what you're doing out here?"

Well, crud on a stick. I was going to have to come up with another lie. It was simply one of those days. "Picking berries." I held up my container for emphasis.

"You can't eat those," Augie pointed out. "They're not for pies or anything. In fact, they're extremely bitter."

Oh, so now he was the berry police. That just figured. "I'm not making a pie."

"What are you making?"

"Lotion." That seemed like a safe enough answer. In fact ... yes. I was known for being kooky and going organic when necessary. Sure, I ate a mixture of potatoes and ground meat product out of cans, but I was still organically minded. "I want to make my own lotion." I warmed to the lie. "These berries are supposed to be great at smoothing skin."

"Uh-huh." Augie didn't look convinced. "Who were you talking to?"

"Myself."

"Do you often walk around the woods talking to yourself?"

If it was one thing I hated it was being put on the spot. It was time to the turn the tables. "And what are you doing out here?" I challenged, wiping my hands on my pants as I stood. "Shouldn't you be protecting the resort guests in the wake of this morning's murder?"

"Abigail hasn't declared it a murder yet."

"Oh, come on!" I made an exaggerated face. "There's no way that woman fell and hit her head the way Buddy wants us to believe. You can't possibly be leaning that way."

"I don't know which way I'm leaning." Augie tilted his head to the side, distraction evident. "Are you alone out here?"

"Do you see anyone else?"

"No, but I heard your voice. It sounded as if you were having a conversation with someone. In fact, that's the reason I'm out here. Two of the guests swear up and down they heard people talking in the woods. They were obviously agitated after what happened to Blair Whitney, but I decided to check."

"Yes, I can't blame them for that." I cursed my bad luck and prepared to paint myself as the crazy sort who talks to thin air until Swoops dropped down three branches and made his presence known by hooting. He was providing me with a very convenient escape hatch. "If you must know, I was talking to Swoops."

"Swoops?" Augie furrowed his brow. "Who is ... oh." His gaze landed on my preening bat and he clucked his tongue. "You brought your little ... friend ... here with you. I should've realized."

Yes, Swoops and I are quite the pair around town. We are as notorious as Zola and her skunk, Kenna and her pink armadillo, and Evian and her fat little frog. Everyone talks about us and we pretend we don't care. As long as they never suspect the truth, everything is fine. It doesn't matter how eccentric everyone believes us to be.

"I don't go anywhere without Swoops." I faked a smile for the annoying creature as he pranced along a tree branch and shifted closer to Augie. "He's like family."

"He's something." Augie stared hard at my familiar. "You

know, most people don't have pet bats. That's not a thing. Why don't you get a cat or something?"

I pictured the hairless cat with his annoying pearls of wisdom and shuddered. "I don't want a cat. This island is crawling with cats. I like my bat."

Swoops made a big show of blowing me kisses when Augie turned his head in my direction. When Augie quickly shifted back to see what Swoops was doing – the creature's claws making noise against the tree branch causing him to alert on the sound – the bat pretended to perch there gazing adoringly at him. The effect was distressing.

"He's definitely tame," Augie noted after a beat. "For a bat, I mean."

"Yes, he's a real people pleaser."

"And he doesn't have rabies, right?"

Swoops looked offended at the statement, but I shot him a warning look when it seemed as if he might try to snatch some of Augie's hair. "He doesn't have rabies."

"Well, that's good." Augie cast another dubious look around the clearing and then exhaled heavily. "I guess I can tell the guests that a murderer isn't running around the woods. Just a deranged former nun with a pet bat. That should make them feel better."

"I'm not a former nun."

"You were going to nun school." Augie just couldn't let that little tidbit go. He'd been fixated on it for thirteen years. It was beyond annoying. "That's pretty much the same thing as being a nun."

Not even close. "Whatever." I tugged on my limited patience and forced a smile. "If that's all, I have work to do."

"Are you going to keep talking to your bat?"

"Probably."

"Okay then." Augie looked reticent as he edged toward the path back to the resort. "Be careful out here, Skye. If you're right, there very well might be a murderer hanging around these woods. I would hate for something to happen to you."

He almost sounded sincere. "Don't worry about me. I can take care of myself."

"Just ... be careful. If you come across someone you don't recognize or trust, take off. Don't be you and pick a fight. I'm serious."

"So am I. I'm fine. You don't have to worry about me."

"It would be nice if that were true." Augie trudged toward the path. "By the way, I know you sweet talked Dylan out of guest records. You'd better hope I don't catch you with them because I could press charges for theft if I wanted to do it."

Ugh. Of course he'd bring that up. "I have no idea what you're talking about." I blinded him with a sweet smile. "Have a nice day."

"I intend to."

Seven

It took me thirty minutes to collect all the berries. Witches were the only ones interested in what they could offer, so I wasn't worried about people complaining about my efforts. My fellow witchy sisters were another story. Of course, we were always fighting anyway, so there was no point in worrying about that. If it wasn't one thing it was another ... and it was always their fault. For the record, I'm an absolute delight.

Swoops settled in his hammock the second we returned to the house, snoring within minutes. He didn't seem bothered in the least about our close call with Augie. I wasn't sure what to make of it. Augie probably figured I was a loon who spent afternoons in the woods talking to her pet bat. That was actually better than the alternative – that I was an elemental witch who talked to sarcastic and judgmental trees next to a brook that could make flora and fauna drunk – so I would simply have to deal with it.

After mixing the batch of truth serum I turned in for the night. I didn't remember the hole in the kitchen door until the next morning when I woke to what looked like a hairless monkey staring into my eyes.

"Son of a ... !" I scrambled to dislodge the beast, which I knew to be a cat, yet hated all the same. I considered myself an animal lover under normal circumstances, but cats are supposed to have hair. I don't care that Tut is a special breed and would be treated as a king or god in certain societies. I seriously couldn't stand him. "Do you knock?"

"I don't have opposable thumbs." Unlike Swoops, Tut could speak out loud. There were times he spoke in front of humans, refusing to care that he risked blowing our cover.

"That doesn't mean you can't knock," I grumbled, running a hand through my snarled hair and glaring at him. "You have a head. Use that to beat on the door."

"That seems a waste of time." Tut swished his tail as he glanced around my messy bedroom. I wasn't much of a housekeeper, and hiring a maid was out of the question given the fact that I lived with a bat and a skunk came and went with the wind. "What are you cooking for breakfast?"

He had to be joking. "Nothing for you."

Corned beef hash.

I couldn't see Swoops, but he was close. Obviously he'd been listening. He'd never admit it – he was supposed to be a brave familiar, after all – but he was terrified of the hairless sphinx. He wasn't the only one.

"You had corned beef hash yesterday," I snapped. "You're getting fat. You're having berries for breakfast."

Corned beef hash. Swoops sounded mournful.

"I said no!"

"You're a very unpleasant human." Tut set about washing himself in a very rude place. "You should try being nicer. You might be surprised how your outlook on life changes when you adjust your attitude."

"I'm fine being known as the witchy one in town." I

meant it. "What are you doing here? I hate it when you sneak into my house and wake me by staring."

"Why do you think I do it?" Tut switched to washing his flank. "You're so easy to rile that I get my jollies."

"Yeah, yeah, yeah." I leaned to the left and peered into the hallway, making a face when I realized Swoops was hanging from the door frame. "Did you clean up the living room?"

Corned beef hash.

I held up a hand. "I'm done talking to you. Corned beef hash is off the menu until you clean up the mess you let Clover make. You're supposed to protect my inner sanctum, not allow attitudinal skunks free rein to wander around with my underwear."

"Oh, did Clover do that?" Tut stopped washing. "I thought maybe your housekeeping skills had deteriorated even further. That's a relief."

"Yes, I know you would've lost sleep over it." I trudged to the door. "Speaking of free rein, you run around town most hours of the day. You wouldn't know where I can find Mitzi Montgomery this morning, would you?"

"Why?"

"I need to talk to her."

"About what?"

"It's none of your concern."

Tut merely stared at me, unblinking, and waited for me to crumble.

"I'm serious." I tried to be stern. If I didn't let these crazy familiars know who was boss they'd start to take over my life. No one wanted that. "I need to know where she is and you don't need to know why."

"Then I don't need to help you," Tut shot back.

Ugh. I knew he'd react that way. I should have been expecting it. "Fine. I'll include you in breakfast if you tell me."

Corned beef hash.

I ignored Swoops and kept my eyes on Tut. "I don't want to have to look for her. I have an important mission today."

"Yes, I know. You're investigating a murder that may not be a murder." Tut was nonchalant. "I know where she'll be in an hour. I'm sure it would be a good location for whatever you have planned. But I won't tell you without something in exchange."

"You're going to say 'corned beef hash,' aren't you?" I was resigned.

Tut shook his wizened head. "I want pancakes ... with blueberries."

And corned beef hash.

"Fine." I was barely awake and my day already sucked. "Pancakes it is."

Corned beef hash.

"I will make you live in a can of corned beef hash if you don't shut up, Swoops. I mean it! I'm the boss."

Apparently I was the only one who believed that.

AFTER FEEDING THE bat and the cat blueberry pancakes and corned beef hash I made my way to the park by the library. It seemed Mitzi was in the midst of another craft bonanza and was adding painting to her list of skills. At least that's what Tut told me, and sure enough, he was right.

I found her on a large expanse of grass, completely alone, a brush in her hand. She had an easel set up, a half-painted canvas resting on it. It looked as if she was painting a landscape, although I'd seen three-year-olds with more talent.

"Hey, Mitzi."

She jumped at the sound of my voice, whipping around and allowing a fearful expression to wash over her features until she regained control. "W-what are you doing here?"

"I came to see you. I even brought a peace offering." I handed her a mug of coffee from the shop around the corner – I asked the girl behind the counter to fix Mitzi's drink of choice – and smiled as she tentatively accepted it. "It's a triple, venti, half sweet, non-fat, caramel macchiato." I had no idea what any of that meant, but I'd memorized it before leaving the coffee shop. "I wanted to apologize for the way I shook you down yesterday."

"You did?" Mitzi's perfectly-plucked eyebrow winged up. "I can't remember you ever apologizing to me. I mean ... like, ever."

"I admit when I'm wrong." I'm rarely wrong so I can say that with a straight face. "I was wrong to be so aggressive with you yesterday. You have to understand, I was shaken up. I tripped over the body myself and I had trouble settling." I had practiced the lie in the mirror five times until I'd finally managed to find a way to deliver it without looking as if I was smelling something akin to rancid pickle farts. "I was upset, but I shouldn't have taken it out on you."

I watched Mitzi closely for signs she suspected I was lying, but she seemed to relax quickly. "Oh, well, that's okay." She sipped her coffee and smiled. "I can see how that would've been upsetting for you. I would've cried if it happened to me." Another sip. One more and I would be good to start drilling her for information. The truth serum worked almost instantaneously. "Thank you for apologizing."

"Don't mention it." I shifted closer to the easel and stared at the canvas. "This is good work. It looks as if you've been practicing." And the lies kept rolling off my tongue with ease. "I didn't know you were interested in painting."

"Oh, I've always been interested in visual arts." There it was. The final sip. "I like to be able to put my feelings and emotions on canvas so others can recognize what I was feeling at any particular moment. It's the inner artist in me. She's ... ravenous."

"Yeah, yeah, yeah." I was quickly losing interest. "It sounds fascinating. So, tell me the whole truth about Buddy and Blair."

Mitzi froze in place, blinking rapidly. She clearly didn't expect the change in my demeanor. Now that she was under the thrall of the truth serum, she didn't have any choice but to answer. "I ... what?"

"Have another drink," I instructed.

Mitzi did as I ordered, her hands shaking as she tried to maintain control of her emotions.

"Now tell me about Buddy and Blair," I repeated. I wasn't in the mood to waste an entire afternoon talking about artistic feelings with Mitzi Montgomery. I wanted answers and then space. "You were hiding something yesterday. I want to know what it is."

"I wasn't ... I mean ... I didn't mean to ... I ... ." Mitzi's eyes filled with alarm when she realized that the lies she was prepared to tell wouldn't come out. She couldn't speak unless it was to tell the truth. She would be forced to undergo brief bouts of pain if she tried. It was one of the serum's little quirks.

"Don't fight it," I chastised. It didn't matter what I told her, she wouldn't remember after the fact. That was another thing I loved about this particular truth serum. The only ones who remembered after being subjugated were other witches. "Just tell me. What's the deal with Buddy and Blair?"

Mitzi fought answering for another full minute, but ultimately gave in. "I always hated that stupid woman." She positively dripped with vitriol, which I found interesting. "You have no idea how terrible she was."

"I'd love to hear about it." I futzed with Mitzi's paint

palette but wasn't cruel enough to mess with her painting. Even I have my limits. "How did Buddy and Blair meet?"

"I already told you. They met in college." Mitzi was obviously frustrated about her loose lips, but she continued talking. "They dated in college, but if you hear Blair tell it now it was only one date even though they really spent an entire semester together."

"Who told you that?"

"Buddy."

"Maybe he was lying and Blair was telling the truth," I suggested. "Have you considered that?"

"Of course not. Buddy is many things, but he's not a liar. In fact, he's militant about telling the truth. He tells the truth over and over again, even when people are tired of hearing it. He might exaggerate a bit, but he's no liar."

"Just a braggart."

"Definitely a braggart." Mitzi clapped her hands over her mouth, horrified by what had spilled out.

"Don't worry about it." I waved off her horror. "You won't even remember in an hour."

"Why is that?"

"Because I said so. Go back to Buddy and Blair. I'm surprised they stayed in touch over the years if they dated for only a semester. That hardly seems the basis for a lasting friendship."

"Oh, they weren't in touch until about four years ago." Mitzi dropped her hands and her expression turned dark. "Then, out of nowhere, Blair came calling. I bet you can't guess why." She looked smug.

"Buddy is the mayor of a very small town that has exactly one claim to fame," I replied, "an expensive resort that a woman addicted to plastic surgery would just love to visit. I'll bet she was hoping he could get her a deal on the procedures."

Mitzi's mouth dropped open. "How do you know that?"

"I'm smarter than I look."

"You'd have to be."

I noticed Mitzi didn't act embarrassed when she said what she really thought about me. Apparently she was only upset that Buddy might find out. What I knew wasn't particularly worrisome. Ah, if she only knew the truth.

"Did Blair and Buddy have regular meetings when she came to the island? I understand she was a seasonal sprucer. That means she visited four times a year. Did she meet up with Buddy each time?"

Mitzi scowled. "Yes. I don't know if he insisted or she did, but they had lunch each visit. They reminisced about old times. Blair put on a big show about how she screwed up by letting Buddy get away. It was ... annoying."

"Were you invited to these meetings?"

"I was invited to the first one, but Buddy said I made Blair uncomfortable because I was jealous. I mean ... as if. She's twenty years older than me and spends all her time recovering from plastic surgery. Why would I be jealous of her?"

I almost felt sorry for Mitzi. Her life obviously hadn't turned out as she thought it would. Being married to Buddy had to be some sort of karmic punishment. There was no other explanation. Still, she stood by him. For a man like Buddy to make his wife feel less than she was seemed almost cruel.

"You had no reason to be jealous of her," I agreed without hesitation. "Buddy should thank his lucky stars that you actually lower yourself to share a bed with him every night."

"Exactly!"

I bit back a smile. "As for Buddy and Blair, was there any talk of her leaving her husband for Buddy?"

Instead of reacting with anger – which I expected – Mitzi

burst into raucous laughter. "Oh, you're so adorable. I can't believe you think that. That's not how Blair works. She wasn't interested in Buddy. She was interested in the perks he could provide. Trust me, if he ran out of twenty-five-percent-off passes she would've run out of time to visit with him."

That actually made sense. "Why didn't Buddy admit to knowing her at the resort yesterday?"

"He was upset. He didn't want to believe it was her. He also didn't want to break down in public. That's not his way."

That wasn't the answer I was expecting. "Did Buddy have a rough night?"

"He drank all day and passed out early. He has a heckuva hangover today."

"And you don't think Buddy killed her?" I had to ask the question. I'd gone this far. There was no turning back. "That's not possible?"

Mitzi was legitimately appalled. "Of course not. Buddy is a big teddy bear. He would never physically hurt anyone."

"Not even if he felt he was being used for a break on plastic surgery?"

"Never." Mitzi was adamant. "Never ever."

"Okay." Goddess help me, I believed her. "So you're saying Buddy wasn't trying to be cagey yesterday. He was simply caught off guard and didn't know how to react."

"That's exactly it. He wasn't trying to hide anything. Why would he? I mean, be honest, do you really think Buddy could've chased down a healthy woman and bashed her over the head with a rock?"

She had a point. "No. I get what you're saying." I licked my lips and took a step back. "Thanks for sharing so much interesting information. I greatly appreciate it."

"I still don't know why I did it."

"That's okay. You won't even remember doing it in a little bit." I offered her a half-wave before heading for the coffee shop. I'd gotten the information I needed out of Mitzi, but it appeared to be a dead end. Even if Buddy felt used, that wasn't a very strong motive for murder ... especially when the victim had a better one sharing a vacation with her. The mistress was the obvious choice. Now I only had to track her down and sucker her into taking a drink from me.

That wouldn't be so hard, right?

Right?

Eight

I was happy to leave Mitzi to her painting. I was fairly certain fuming would be involved in that endeavor – at least until the serum wore off – so I was happy to make my escape. My next stop was the resort to track down the mistress and daughter and dose them, but I figured it was probably wise to stop by the front desk first.

Dylan was there, just as I expected. Instead of lighting up when he saw me, he made a cross with his fingers and extended it in my direction. "Go away. I don't want to talk to you."

"Aren't crosses supposed to keep vampires away?" I hunted through the mint bowl on the counter and came back with a green one. "I'm not a vampire."

"You are a blood-sucking fiend."

It seemed he was still upset. I would have to fix that. "You're coming to karaoke tonight, right?"

Dylan lowered his fingers, but only a bit. "Of course. It's Friday night. Where else would I go?"

"Well, I just want you to know that I'm really looking forward to our dance." That was the biggest lie of all. I hate dancing. I'm rhythmically challenged. Plus, well, Dylan makes sighing sounds whenever he manages to get one of us out on the dance floor. He's like a teenage girl who finally gets a chance to dance with her crush and somehow ends up pretty in pink or something. No, seriously. I swear I saw that in a movie once.

"Really?" Dylan brightened. "Are you just saying that because you don't want me to be angry with you any longer?"

I honestly didn't care if Dylan was angry – at least under normal circumstances. I did care if he was angry enough to cut me off from information, though. "I really am." I forced a bright smile. "I'm sorry that Augie came down on you. You have to understand, that's not because of you or me. That's because he's Augie and he takes joy in making others miserable."

"Oh, I don't think ... ." Dylan trailed off and let his eyes snag on something over my shoulder. I knew without turning around that it was Augie.

"Mr. Taylor, I hope you know that I wasn't saying that about you." Dylan sounded downright terrified. "I respect you far too much to ever say anything behind your back."

"Way to be brave, Dylan." I clapped him on the shoulder before swiveling to find Augie, hands on hips and frown on lips, staring at me. "Hello, Augie."

"My name is August." His tone was clipped. "No one calls me Augie. You're the only one who insists on doing it, and I want you to stop."

That was a damnable lie. Everyone in town called him Augie. That was his nickname as a child and it stuck. No matter how badly he wanted to shake it, it simply wasn't going to happen.

"Does your mother still call you 'Augie the froggy'?"

Augie scowled. "She never called me that!"

"I distinctly remember her calling you that."

"You called me that when you wanted to irritate me," Augie corrected. "My mother would never call me that because she's a saint. I mean ... an actual saint."

I sobered despite myself. Rumor had it Augie's mother was battling an illness they were trying to keep quiet. Augie's sister moved from Eternal Springs more than a decade before, which left Augie as his mother's only caregiver after his father died shortly after Augie finished high school. Bringing Augie's mother into our continuing bickering probably wasn't the smartest — or nicest — idea.

"I'm sorry." I meant it. "I shouldn't have teased you about your mother. How is she doing?"

"She's ... fine." Augie averted his gaze and I knew that was a lie. I also knew it wasn't my place to push him.

"I'm still sorry." I forced a smile. "I won't tease you about your mother again. That was out of line and unfair."

"Well ... ."

"There are plenty of other things to tease you about," I added, grinning. "I don't need your mother to mess with your mind."

Augie rolled his eyes and stepped to the desk so he could look at the computer Dylan was using. "You're not giving her information, are you?"

Dylan's shoulders stiffened. "Of course not, sir. You can trust me."

"I would hate to have to fire you," Augie persisted. "Skye is not allowed to poke around our files. No one is allowed to poke around our files. That includes her other little buddies that you have a soft spot for, too."

"I won't let anyone see the records, sir." Dylan sounded like a deranged Army recruit. "I'll guard them with my life."

"Oh, geez!" I blew out a sigh as I scorched Augie with a dark look. "Way to terrorize him, Augie. You're going to give the poor kid a complex."

"I wouldn't need to if you weren't such a busybody."

"I'm not a busybody. I'm a curious soul. Curiosity is good. It means I'm intelligent."

Augie snorted. "What idiot told you that?"

"I tell myself that at least once a week."

"And that's why you're a menace." Augie crossed his arms over his chest as he leaned a hip against the front desk. "What are you doing out here? I would have thought you had your hands full with other things. I mean ... where is your bat? You didn't bring him, did you?"

"Swoops is at home sleeping off a corned beef hash coma," I replied. "No one will see him until nightfall."

"Corned beef hash?" Augie wrinkled his forehead. "Are bats supposed to eat corned beef hash? I thought they ate fruit and bugs."

"Yes, well, Swoops has a refined palate. He's not like normal bats."

"Just like you're not like a normal woman." Augie ran his tongue over his teeth as he regarded me. "You still haven't told me what you're doing here."

"I missed Dylan and wanted to visit him."

Dylan's smile was so wide it almost blinded me.

"Stand down, Dylan." Augie was rueful. "She's messing with you again. We talked about this yesterday. You can't believe anything she says when she's blowing sunshine up your behind."

"I never blow sunshine up anyone's behind," I countered. "It doesn't sound very hygienic."

"Ha, ha." Augie flicked me between the eyebrows, causing me to rear back. "What are you doing here?"

He wasn't going to leave it alone. I had no choice but to 'fess up or leave. Luckily for him, I had two motivations when I decided to visit the resort. I only had to own up to one of them to get out of this.

"I'm here to talk to Abigail. I want to see if she's going to rule Blair Whitney's death an accident or a homicide."

Whatever answer he expected, that wasn't it. "I guess that makes sense. I can answer that question for you. I just came from Abigail's office."

"So, what did she say?"

"She's going with non-conclusive."

I should've seen that coming. "You have got to be kidding me!" It took everything I had to keep from exploding and unleashing a mini-tornado on the room. "You know that means it was murder, right? The simple fact that she can't call it an accident means it was murder."

"I'm well aware." Augie looked distressed by the admission. "I don't think there's any question about the blow being deliberate. I happened to be in there when Abigail took a closer look and there's no way a fall caused that much damage. It looks like Mrs. Whitney was hit at least twice, more likely three times."

Now that right there was interesting. "Have you questioned the mistress?"

Augie narrowed his eyes. "You're not even supposed to know about the mistress."

"I know about a lot of things I'm not supposed to know about."

"That's nothing to brag about."

"I think it depends on where you're standing."

"You just have to have the last word, don't you?" Augie made a disgusted sound in the back of his throat and shook his head. "Skye, I'm not going to let this go. I'm going to do my job. You're a reporter. It's not your job to solve murders."

"Who says I'm trying to solve a murder?"

"I know you."

Sadly, he knew me better than most. It was an uncomfortable feeling. "I'm not trying to solve a murder. I'm merely trying to get information. I need to play up what a wonderful woman Blair Whitney was in my article, after all. It needs to be a celebration of her life, not a commentary on her death."

I thought it was a positively brilliant way to go. Augie didn't fall for it. Instead he leaned closer and wagged a warning finger in my face. "Don't stick your nose in this. That's the last thing I need."

"Did I say I was going to stick my nose in this?"

"No, but you never admit when you're about to do wrong. Instead you pretend it's all a misunderstanding ... even if you're sitting in the back of a cop cart when you're denying being up to no good as the golf course sprinklers spray red water all over the place so it looks as if a massacre happened on the grounds."

Ugh! I can't believe he brought up that incident. It happened, like, ten years ago. I was young and dumb ... and, well, drunk ... at the time. "I still maintain I didn't do that. I think the sprinklers were temporarily possessed."

"Right." Augie made an exaggerated face. "I am warning you. If you stick your nose into this you won't like it when I yank it out."

"I'll keep that in mind."

"You do that."

I WAITED UNTIL I WAS SURE Augie was otherwise engaged – and by that, I mean he was mediating a squabble between three of the maids, all of whom looked as if they wanted to smother him with their boobs to see who the ultimate winner would be – before slipping into the spa area of the resort. I was familiar with the layout, and what I would have to do to gain entrance.

Without batting an eyelash I pressed my hands to my face, whispered a small spell and ran my hands over my hair as my features changed. I saw my new appearance as I passed the mirrors on the wall. My new look was young and chic, matching one of the masseuse's I knew was in the parking lot dealing with a car issue that I may or may not have instigated. I didn't have much time to get answers, but I had more than a few minutes to poke around.

To be fair, I didn't really change my looks. It's more that I enacted a glamour, and the image others saw was what I wanted them to see. It was a fun bit of magic I'd mastered in high school. It had come in handy a time or two since then, mostly because Augie was right; I am a busybody. Sometimes I simply want to know things. I can't help it. That's why I became a journalist.

"Hey, Margo."

It took me a moment to realize the secretary behind the desk was talking to me as I passed. I offered a lame hand salute that caused her to make a face. I pretended it was all totally normal and slipped into the hallway leading to the massage rooms. I was familiar enough with the layout to know where I needed to go.

I stopped in front of the board on the wall and mentally flipped through the three names listed. I didn't care about the first two, but the third was a different story.

Lena Preston. She was the mistress's mother in our tangled web of family intrigue. She was still at the resort – although if I were her I would've bolted the day before – and she was in desperate need of some massage therapy. The good thing about that is massages make women chatty ... especially if you gave them a magical jolt. Just think of it as witchy acupuncture and don't dwell on the ethics too much.

The room was dark when I let myself in, the only light coming from a small nightlight in the corner. The room was wired with speakers so that relaxation music – the sort of stuff that sounds like ocean waves beating flutes to death on rocky shorelines – filled the room as I moved closer to the table in the center of the space.

Lena was already face down under the sheet, her eyes pressed shut, and she was clearly waiting for her massage to start.

"I want the hot stone massage today, Margo," she murmured. "My muscles are extremely tense."

"Yes, ma'am." I had no intention of actually rubbing the woman, instead planting a suggestion that I was so she would open up. I made a big show of squirting massage oil on my hands before leaning close to her ear and whispering. "Somnum."

It was a simple spell, one of the few Latin words I remembered from my classes at St. Joan of Arc. I waited a beat until I heard Lena murmur something under her breath and then I jumped right in. Margo would only be distracted by her car issues for another ten minutes tops, which meant I had to be out of the room long before that.

"What's the deal with your daughter and Blair Whitney?"

Lena didn't act surprised by the question. "They hate each other."

"Because your daughter is sleeping with Mrs. Whitney's husband? You know that's the rumor, right?"

"It's not a rumor. I encouraged her to do it."

I was dumbfounded. "Why?"

"Charles Whitney III is a very rich man." Lena was matter-of-fact. "He's worth billions. Not millions, but billions."

"He's still married."

"Not happily." Lena made a face as she shifted slightly on the table. "Blair was an unpleasant woman and didn't care about meeting Charles' needs. When Charles started showing interest in Rebecca, she came to me with her concerns. We talked about the issue and agreed it would probably be in everyone's best interests if she allowed him to make a move."

I had trouble wrapping my head around Lena's blasé attitude. "So you basically prostituted your daughter."

"I did not!" Lena's voice shook. "We made a decision that was best for our family. We're still convinced it will work out."

"Right." I felt as if I'd accidentally tripped and fell into an alternate dimension. "Why did Blair Whitney invite you on this trip?"

"Because she knew Charles was in love with Rebecca and didn't want them spending any time together while she was getting one of her nip-and-tucks. This was simply her way of controlling the situation."

"And because you didn't want her pushing the issue, you agreed," I surmised. "That's just ... all screwed up."

"Tell me about it." Lena didn't appear bothered by my judgment. "We all knew it would be an uncomfortable situation, but no one thought it would end this way."

She gave me an opening for my next question, so I took it. "Did your daughter kill Blair?"

Lena snorted. "Of course not! My daughter is many things, but she's no murderer."

"Okay." I licked my lips. "Did you kill Blair Whitney?"

"No. I'm not a murderer either. You're looking at it wrong. Blair was notorious for self-medicating. She drank herself into a stupor every night. She added pills to the mix regularly. She wasn't killed. She tripped and hit her head. It was an accident that we all saw coming years ago."

I stared at the woman's back for a long time. The spell I'd cast wasn't exactly a truth spell. It was supposed to make the individual under it feel relaxed enough to spill whatever came to mind. That didn't mean lies were out of the question. I was almost out of time and dosing Lena with truth serum now was too risky.

"Do you feel guilty about any of this?" I took a step toward the door as I ran the information about Blair through my head. It would make sense that she was self-medicating. Her life was falling apart around her and she wanted to forget. Still, an accident didn't fit the facts of the case. Something else was going on here.

"Why would I feel guilty?" Lena challenged. "Blair didn't give her husband what he needed and my daughter did. There's nothing wrong with that."

I could think of a few things wrong with it, but decided to let it go. I was out of time. "Oh, just one more thing." I paused with my hand on the door handle. "I think you should go to Coconuts bar and participate in karaoke with your daughter tonight."

It was a basic suggestion that Lena could accept or deny. I hoped she was relaxed enough to simply agree.

"We're not karaoke people."

I scowled. I wasn't a karaoke person either. I decided to try a different tack. "They have the best rum runners in town. They're strong ... and cheap."

Lena's demeanor changed in a heartbeat. "That sounds fun."

"Yeah. I thought that might pique your interest."

Nine

Karaoke at Coconuts is one of those weekly traditions that I'm embarrassed to admit I attend. I can't sing. I'm a terrible dancer. And, as much as I love bad seventies and eighties music there's nothing more annoying than listening to the same people belt out the same lame tunes week after week. I mean ... there's only so many times you can hear "Summer Nights" before wishing the singers would actually disappear in a flying car.

I had no choice but to attend tonight. I had a plan and I wanted to stick to it.

By the time I entered the bar, opting for simple cargo pants and a black shirt, it was packed with regulars. Tourists almost always find their way to the bar – it's too loud to ignore – but regulars pack the seats and turn it into a gossip free-for-all.

I found Kenna, Evian, and Zola sitting at a table in the corner. Even though we like to bicker, we also make a show of hanging out because that way people don't question us when a situation that requires pooled witchy energy arises. We were left behind for a reason – to clean up the mess we wrought as teenagers – and the occasional issue continued to crop up. We were resigned to working together, even though it wasn't always comfortable.

"I see you guys are all dressed up." I wrinkled my nose at their sparkly outfits and ornate sandals. "It's just karaoke, for crying out loud."

"I always feel good when I look good," Kenna shot back, her hair so glossy it gleamed under the seashell twinkle lights. "You should try it some time."

"Yeah, yeah." I waved off her dig. "So, I got some information on the dead woman at the resort today. It seems she was quite the busy little bee."

Zola, a rum runner in hand, raised her eyebrows as she sipped. "Does this have something to do with what I told you?"

"Kind of." I related my afternoon, leaving nothing out. When I was done, instead of being impressed, my former classmates were amused.

"You need a hobby or something," Evian suggested. "Have you considered taking up yoga or dance classes? If anyone ever needed to sweat out her aggression, it's you."

I blew a raspberry in her direction as I signaled the waitress for a drink. It was karaoke night, so there was only one thing on tap for the regulars. It was no big deal for me because I liked rum runners. I simply had to remind myself that they were stronger than they tasted because there's nothing worse than a drunk witch on karaoke night.

"I have a hobby."

"Since when?"

"Well ... I haven't killed you guys yet. That's got to count as the most benevolent of hobbies, right?"

Kenna let loose a low whistle as she shook her head. "Who crawled in your corned beef hash and died?"

"It's just been a long day." That was true. "I think I talked the mistress's mother into bringing everyone here so I can squeeze more information out of them. I'm antsy."

"And why would you want that?"

"Because Blair Whitney was murdered and I want to know who did it. I'd think you would feel the same way because tourism is literally your job. If people believe we have a murderer on the loose they'll stop coming to the island."

Kenna leaned back in her chair and gave me an appraising look. For a brief moment I thought she was going to agree with me. That had never happened before. It turned out it wasn't going to happen now either. "If I thought you were actually worried about tourism I might cut you some slack," she said. "You're only interested in getting information because you're a busybody."

She said that like it was a bad thing. "Whatever. The simple fact of the matter is that as concerned residents we should want to make sure that no one gets away with murder on our watch."

Instead of responding, Kenna ducked her head under the table. I watched her for a moment, confused, and when she popped back up I pinned her with a look.

"What are you doing?"

"Looking for the pile of crap you're clearly shoveling. I thought it might be invisible."

"Oh, whatever." I rolled my neck and kicked back in my chair. "I stand by what I said. I'm a community-minded individual and I want my community to be safe."

"Says the woman who allows her familiar to run around town crapping in people's coffee when they're not looking," Evian drawled.

"That is a community service all its own."

"How?"

I was about to launch into a ridiculous explanation for my stance, but my attention was diverted by the group of women walking into the bar. I recognized Lena, as well as her daughter, right away. I'd seen photographs, although they weren't altogether flattering. The two other women were harder for me to gauge. "Well, look who decided to stop by after all."

Three heads snapped in the direction I stared. I didn't miss the little hiss Zola allowed to escape when she realized I hadn't been kidding about inviting a possible murderer to karaoke night.

"I can't believe they showed up." Kenna made a clucking sound as she shook her head. "That seems rather inappropriate, don't you think? I mean ... the one woman's mother was found dead in the bushes thirty-six hours ago. I don't think most people grieve the loss of their mother with rum runners."

That sounded like the best way to grieve. "Do you know which one she is? I only saw photos of Lena and Rebecca."

"The blonde," Zola answered automatically. "I saw her in the coffee shop earlier today and someone pointed her out to me. Her name is Sheridan."

"Sheridan Whitney?" I made a face. "What is it with these people and their preppy names?"

"I think it goes along with money," Evian supplied. "Like ... if you make more than three million a year you get a different baby name book than everyone else."

That actually didn't sound out of the realm of possibility. I studied the woman in question for a long time, doing my best to wrap my head around her bland expression. She didn't seem moved by anything going on around her. Granted, she wasn't laughing and enjoying herself. She didn't exactly look prostrate with grief or anything either. "She doesn't exactly look like a woman in mourning, does she?"

"Why?" Kenna challenged. "Is it because she's not wearing black?"

I would never be that shallow. "No. She just looks ... normal."

"Maybe she's in shock," Zola offered. "She didn't say much at the coffee shop. She sort of sat and listened as the other woman — the one with the brown hair sticking close to her — did most of the talking."

I switched my attention to the fourth woman. "That would be the assistant, right?"

"Yes. Her name is Jane Smith."

I pressed my lips together to keep from laughing. "I take it back. The preppy names are better than Jane Smith. I mean ... there are worse names than Sheridan."

"She's the assistant," Kenna pointed out. "Her name is supposed to be boring so she doesn't overshadow everyone else."

"So ... you're basically saying that no one named Bambi has ever wanted to be a secretary."

"I think if you name your kid Bambi that she's got another life already carved out for her," Kenna said. "Sadly, it's probably on a stripper pole ... or maybe that's simply how it always seems to work out."

"Maybe." I watched the women for another moment before downing my drink in four long swigs and getting to my feet. "I'll be back in a little bit."

"Oh, I don't like the look in your eyes," Evian complained. "You're about to do something stupid, aren't you?"

"Would I do that?"

Kenna, Evian, and Zola nodded in unison, causing me to scowl.

"I never do anything stupid," I shot back. "I'm a master at getting information and hurting no one in the process."

"Yeah, I'll remind you of that when you get arrested for doing something dopey and are locked in the back of the cop cart," Kenna said. "By the way, if that happens, I'm not bailing you out."

"Me either," Zola enthusiastically added. She was clearly already halfway to drunk.

"I might bail you out," Evian offered. "I'll charge you interest, though."

"I'm so glad I've been stuck with all of you on this rotten island," I muttered, grabbing my purse and slinging the strap over my head so I'd have easy access to what I'd hidden inside when I got behind the bar. "Your loyalty and friendship touches my very soul."

"Something else might end up touching you if you get arrested," Kenna shot back, grabbing the song book from the end of the table and flipping it open. "So ... who wants to sing 'Love Shack' with me tonight?"

Ugh. I was glad to get away from that discussion.

I SPENT THE NEXT TWENTY minutes behind the bar with Bonnie Fisher, one of Coconuts' most popular bartenders. She was in her forties, didn't get territorial about the space behind the bar and was always up for telling a good story ... whether it was true or not.

"I swear on my mother's life that I saw it." Bonnie mimed crossing her hand over her heart, her expression solemn. I'd come up with a solid plan for getting the truth serum into Lena and her friends. Unfortunately, I had to listen to Bonnie's tale of terror about running into Bigfoot on her way to work to get access to the liquor.

"Are you sure it wasn't just Jim Oleson?" I queried. "He's got that back-hair situation and his beard gets pretty bushy if he goes without trimming it every few days."

Bonnie made an exaggerated face. "I'm sure it wasn't Jim Oleson. It was Bigfoot."

I held up my hands in capitulation. "Sorry. It was Bigfoot. I stand corrected."

"He's out there, and the government knows about it." Bonnie lowered her voice to a conspiratorial whisper. "He's part of their black files."

I had no idea what she meant by "black files." I also didn't care. "Well, if you see him again, try to get a photograph. I'll totally print it in The Town Croaker and give you a photo credit."

Bonnie mock saluted. "You've got it."

I mixed four rum-runners and left them on a tray as I escaped from behind the bar long enough to approach Dylan. He sat with several of his co-workers and I didn't miss the looks he lobbed my way when a slow song started. "I'll have time to dance a little later," I offered as I neared. "I just have to finish up with some drinks first. It shouldn't be long."

Dylan broke out in a wide smile. "Okay." He looked younger than his twenty years when he blushed, if that was even possible. "You look pretty tonight." I hadn't worn the requested dress, but he didn't seem to care.

"Thank you." I straightened and cast a glance to Lena and her cohorts. They seemed deep in conversation and were almost finished with their first round of drinks. It was the perfect time to deliver my round of special libations – the ones I'd dosed with truth serum – and get them talking. Things were falling into place.

"And we meet again."

I jolted when Augie slid into the open spot to my right and graced me with what I'm sure he considered a charming grin. He had a rum runner in each hand and looked as if he'd dressed up for the occasion ... and by that I mean he'd put on a fresh polo shirt.

"We really do need to stop meeting like this," I drawled,

rolling my eyes when he handed me one of the rum runners. "What's this?"

"I bought you a drink."

"You bought me a ... ." I trailed off, dumbfounded. "Why? You've never bought me a drink before."

"Maybe I thought you looked like you needed one."

Was that an insult? "I ... um ... ." For lack of anything better to do, I accepted the drink and drank half of it so I had time to collect my thoughts. "This is great. Thank you."

"You're welcome." Augie's lips curved as he looked toward the bar. "Is that Shana Witherspoon doing 'Redneck Woman' again?"

I nodded without looking at the stage. "She does that song every week. I don't know why you're surprised."

"I'm not surprised. I just thought maybe she'd branch out one week."

"I sincerely doubt that will ever happen. I'm pretty sure she only knows the one song."

"Someone is feeling catty." Augie made mock growling sounds and pretended to flick imaginary cat paws. "Rawr."

"Oh, don't do that," I complained. "People will think you're gay and you already have enough strikes against you when it comes to finding a date in this town."

Augie's smile slipped. "You don't always have to say what comes to your mind. You know that, right?"

"Maybe I like being blunt."

"And maybe it's a defense mechanism because you're afraid to get close to people," Augie suggested. "In fact ... ." He grabbed the drink from my hand and slid it onto a nearby table, depositing his there as well before dragging me toward the dance floor.

At first I was confused. Then I felt something else that I couldn't quite identify. It felt like panic. "What are you doing?"

"We're dancing." He didn't ask. He didn't extend a hand and wait for me to accept it. Instead he simply slid his arms around me and started swaying to the music. I was absolutely befuddled.

"We don't dance." I pushed against his chest – which felt much more solid than it should – as I tried to find an escape hatch. "We've never danced."

"There's a first time for everything." Augie ignored my efforts to push him away and glanced around the bar as we circled. "I see our victim's daughter is here with the other members of that little group. What do you make of that?"

"Am I supposed to make something of it?"

"They haven't been talkative since the incident."

That was hardly surprising. Of course, I had a plan to break that streak. "Maybe they simply don't want to talk to you. You're head of security. You might intimidate them."

"I'm pretty sure I've never intimidated anyone in my life."

"Still, you're an official presence," I argued. "They might do better trying to talk to me. In fact, I was just putting together a tray of drinks to deliver to them. I was hoping that might loosen their lips a bit." That wasn't a lie even though I conveniently left out the part about dosing the rum runners with truth serum. I flicked my eyes to the bar and my heart skipped a beat when I realized the tray on the counter was bare of the drinks I'd painstakingly mixed. "I ... what happened to the rum runners?"

"Are those the ones from the bar?" Augie asked, his hand flat on the small of my back. He actually seemed to be enjoying this dancing thing, which I didn't get. "Bonnie said you were mixing four drinks for you and your partners in crime. She took three of the drinks to them and I brought the fourth to you."

Uh-oh. "What?" Panic licked my heart and I could feel the blood draining from my face. "She delivered the drinks I

BAT OUT OF SPELL

was mixing to ... ." I couldn't finish the sentence. The idea was so horrible that my brain wanted to shut down. Then the other part of what Augie said penetrated the haze in my busy mind. "You gave me one of the drinks from the tray?"

Augie nodded, smiling down at me as he pressed a bit closer. "You're not so bad when you're not constantly trying to pick a fight with me."

Oh, no. He had a sappy look on his face. "How many drinks have you had?"

"About four. It's been a really long day and it ended on a sour note."

That was so not what I wanted to hear. "Have Kenna and the others drunk from their glasses yet?" I managed to extricate myself from his iron grip and started in that direction as I clung to a last thread of hope. It disappeared in two seconds flat when my three former classmates clinked glasses and downed drinks simultaneously. "Oh, crap!"

"You're kind of soft, too." Augie ran his hand over my back and pulled me back against him. "I don't know why I never noticed that."

"Because I'm not soft. I'm ... hard to be around." And I was now cursed with the inability to lie for the next hour. This was not good. I had to get out of here. "You know what, Augie? I really need to get some air."

"One more song." Augie was in no mood to release me, rum clearly fueling his belief that he felt amorous ... which had to be one of the most ludicrous things I'd ever heard.

"Augie."

"I love this song."

I cringed at the opening bars of "Total Eclipse of the Heart." Unfortunately, I recognized the voice belting out the song before even looking toward the stage. The sight of Kenna with a microphone in her hand – especially when she had no control over song choices – was one of the most truly terrifying things I'd ever seen.

"Ugh. She's going to be so angry."

"I don't really remember her singing this song before." Augie furrowed his brow. "It doesn't seem her style."

"She's a closet fan." I'd heard her sing it back in the day when we shared a bathroom. She denied it, of course, but I always knew the truth. Now everyone in town was going to know the truth. That couldn't possibly be good. "I need to get out of here."

"Not until we're done dancing." Augie was firm. "You even smell good tonight. Did you shower or something?"

Only Augie could manage to slide in an insult when trying to be a drunken lothario. "Ugh. This is going to come back to bite me so hard."

Ten

I woke with a thousand regrets the next morning.

My head throbbed as I stumbled through the living room, barely noticing the bras and panties that remained strewn about, and rubbed my forehead as I waited for the Keurig to brew my coffee. I seriously wished I could throw it straight into my eyes to kick start the waking process, but third-degree retinal burns didn't sound like fun.

It's possible to have a magic hangover, for the record. That's what I struggled with after a night of fighting the truth serum while being passed between Augie and Dylan for dancing purposes. I was on my feet the entire night, and it was only after the truth serum finally passed out of my system – and Kenna, Evian, and Zola grasped exactly why they'd been acting like such goofs and began hunting me – that I realized why I was so popular. The magic I used to expel the truth serum turned it into an aphrodisiac of sorts, apparently making me attractive to every single man in town. The only reason I wasn't fawned over more is because Augie seemed to be marking his territory while glaring at people, sending silent warnings of sorts, and he eventually scared everyone off.

I was mortified by his reaction. We weren't close – we spent all of our time battling, after all – and for him to be all over me the way he was took a strong dose of magic. That was on me. It was my fault. I should've watched the drinks more closely. Not only had I lost a prime opportunity to question my suspect about the murder of her romantic rival, I'd also managed to get various pairs of lips throughout town wagging. I was absolutely positive I'd be answering questions about my relationship with Augie for days, maybe even weeks.

It was humiliating, which meant he'd probably feel doubly bad when he woke today ... and have no idea why it happened in the first place. It wasn't as if he was acting on emotions he buried deep. My efforts to fight the truth serum turned him into a randy devil. I almost felt bad for the embarrassment he'd surely feel.

Almost.

I showered after finishing my coffee and felt nearly human again, although a little draggy, when I returned to the main floor. I'd resigned myself to picking up my own bra and panties because I'd been reduced to wearing the only two things left in my drawers: granny panties and a sports bra. I was readying myself for the task when there was a knock at the door.

I expected irate visits from Kenna, Evian, and Zola before the end of the day, so I didn't bother looking through the peephole before opening the door. They'd find a way to make me pay before darkness descended, so it was probably best to get it over with. Instead of three witchy antagonists, though – or one obnoxious skunk – I found Augie shuffling on the porch. He had two cups of coffee from the downtown shop in his hands.

I was surprised ... and a little unnerved. "Augie."

"Good morning, Skye." Augie swallowed hard as he cautiously met my gaze. "I thought we should talk."

Oh, geez. I should've expected this. Augie was going to accuse me of doing something to him – which I technically had – and we were going to end up in a humongous fight when I lied and denied culpability. This was so not how I wanted to start my day.

"I don't think talking is necessary," I hedged. "I'm not feeling all that hot and if you're here to pick a fight ... ."

"I'm here to apologize," Augie said hurriedly, stealing my breath as he pushed into my house without invitation. He pulled up short when he saw the bra and panty explosion in the living room, absently handing me one of the coffee concoctions as he perused the mess. "What happened here?"

"Would you believe me if I told you that I like it this way?" I didn't consider myself the sort of woman who embarrasses over minor things, but the blush creeping up my cheeks told me I was closer to that sort of woman than I would've liked.

"Not really."

"Swoops did it." I sipped the coffee and almost groaned at the taste. My Keurig was good for delivering a quick jolt of caffeine, but nothing beat the real deal. "He has a thing for my underwear."

I didn't miss the indignant hoot from the second-floor landing, but I refused to look in that direction.

"Your pet bat carries your ... um, undergarments ... around the house?" Augie looked as uncomfortable as I felt. "That's ... different."

"He's a little pervert. What can I say?"

I heard that, and you're going to owe me corned beef hash for life!

I ignored the voice in my head and made a spot for Augie on the couch. I had to move three bras and panties to do it, but I dropped them on the coffee table with as much dignity as I could muster and pretended there was nothing odd about the situation as he got comfortable. "So ... why are you here again?"

"Because I made a fool of myself last night." Augie stared at his shoes rather than me, his mortification evident. "What I did was ... not acceptable."

I racked my brain. "What did you do?"

"I ... danced with you."

"And while a little odd — especially when you wanted me to do 'Baby Got Back' while smacking my own rear end — it wasn't the worst thing I saw all night," I offered. "Don't worry about it."

"Ugh." Augie slapped his hand to his face. "I forgot about 'Baby Got Back.'"

Hmm. "Did you also forget about 'Hit Me With Your Best Shot'?"

I didn't think it was possible, but Augie's face turned an even deeper shade of red. "Yes."

"So, if you didn't come to apologize for either of those sterling numbers, what did you come to apologize about?" Perhaps I'd forgotten something during the long night. Once I realized that dodging my friends was about to become an issue, everything turned into a total blur.

"The rest of it." Augie's voice was soft.

"The rest of what?"

"You know."

I really had no idea. "I don't know, Augie." I felt sorry for him, although I had no idea why. Any other day of the year I would've been celebrating his misery. He was a total pain and had it coming, after all. This, though, this was my fault, and I felt rotten that he seemed to be taking it on himself. "You're going to have to tell me. There are apparently things about last night I don't remember. One of those things is anything you could possibly have to apologize about."

I was purposely giving him an out. Most men would've jumped at the chance to wave goodbye and flee. Augie wasn't most men. He was too much of a gentleman.

"I kept forcing you to dance." Augie swallowed hard as he finally shifted his eyes to mine. "You didn't want to, but I kind of made you."

"You didn't make me." Not exactly. "You pressured me to dance, but I could've gotten out of the situation whenever I wanted. Don't get all worked up about that."

"You kept saying you had to go, but I made you stay."

"And I will be forever appalled by how poorly we sing together." I couldn't stop myself from grinning at his hangdog expression. "It's not the end of the world, Augie. We got a little drunk and danced."

"And sang."

"Yes, well, we're hardly the first people to make fools of ourselves at karaoke night," I pointed out. "Besides, after Evian's rendition of 'Bohemian Rhapsody,' people won't be talking about us." I didn't really believe that. Augie appeared to need his coffee with a side shot of reassuring lies this morning, though.

"Yeah." Augie brightened, although only marginally. "I didn't even know she could headbang."

I was fairly certain Evian didn't either, which was only one of the reasons I was certain she would be coming after me. "She's multi-faceted talented." I sipped my coffee and gave him an appraising look. "As for the other stuff, you didn't really force me. I could've escaped if I'd wanted to." The sobering thing was, that was true. I could've escaped if I'd put a little effort into the maneuver. So why didn't I? "You didn't hurt me or anything. We just ... danced."

"I seem to remember shots and flirting, too." Augie

pressed his lips together. "My memory flakes out after that. We didn't do anything else, did we?"

Wait ... what was he asking? "Are you wondering if we had a quickie in the parking lot or something?"

"I ... no!" Augie vehemently shook his head. "I know you're not that type of person."

"Not last time I checked," I agreed. "So ... what are you asking?"

"We didn't, like ... um ... kiss, did we? I remember being really close to you for a very long time, and I'm hoping we didn't kiss."

Ah, that's what was bothering him. I understood his terror. "No. You don't have to worry about that."

"Good." Augie lowered his forehead to his hands. "I can't imagine finally kissing you and not being able to remember it."

I froze at the way he phrased the comment. "W-what?"

Augie pushed forward as if he hadn't heard my panicked utterance. "I just didn't want you to think that I was the sort of guy who wandered around kissing people without asking first."

"Yes, that would be a true tragedy," I drawled. "I'm sure that would've thrown both of us. You can rest easy. That didn't happen."

"Good." Augie sucked in a breath, and when he looked at me this time he seemed more together and less freaked. "I am sorry about the dancing. I don't know what got into me."

I did, but there was no way I could share my knowledge. "It's okay. I'm sure we'll have to answer a few questions from curious townsfolk over the next few days – or maybe even weeks – but worse things have happened."

"Yeah." Augie's exhale was shaky and deep as he leaned back, shifting a moment and digging in the cushion behind him until he came back with a purple padded bra. "Yours?"

I yanked the bra out of his hand. "Don't bother smirking. It's a bra. It's not as if you've seen me in it or anything. You can't smirk until that happens."

"Until, huh?" Augie's eyes glinted with mischief. I opened my mouth to tell him it would never happen, but he was already turning somber. "I came here for another reason, too."

I snapped my mouth shut as I tilted my head to the side, considering. "You have more on your mind than the fact that you thought you might have kissed me and not remembered it?"

"I do. That was the biggie, but now that you've assured me it didn't happen I can focus on the other bit. You'll probably be more interested in that anyway."

Now I was definitely intrigued. "Okay. I'm all ears."

"You were all hands on my rear during 'Baby Got Back' last night, but I've decided to be magnanimous and let that go." Augie's quick smile was too much to allow my anger to kindle. "Besides, I think you're going to like what I have for you so much you'll forgive me almost anything."

He thought an awful lot about himself if he believed that to be true. "Just tell me why you're here, Augie."

"This." Augie dug in his pocket and came out with a slip of paper.

I wordlessly took it and read aloud. "Room sixteen at the Beachcomber resort." I had no idea what it was supposed to mean. "Are you trying to set up a clandestine meeting with me to see if we can find another duet to sing or something?"

Augie chuckled, the sound low and warm. "No. That's where Charles Whitney is staying."

I knit my eyebrows. "But ... our Beachcomber resort?"

"That would be the one."

"Did he come to the island to claim his wife's body or something?"

"That's just it. He's been here for three days." Augie was deathly serious as he rubbed his palms over his knees. "I got an anonymous tip that he was in town. Someone slipped it under my office door at the resort. I didn't think much of it at first – thought maybe it was a joke or someone trying to send me on a wild goose chase – but I confirmed it last night."

That made absolutely no sense. "Why would he be on the island?"

"I don't know."

"Did his wife know he was here?"

"I don't know."

"What about his mistress?"

"I believe that's how he got caught." Augie was earnest. "Someone saw the mistress going into a room there and Charles was later seen with her. I'm not sure how my anonymous tipster knew who he was, but I have confirmed that he's really here ... and he checked in hours before his wife died."

This development was quite simply unbelievable. "Do you think he killed his wife?"

"I don't know." Augie helplessly held up his hands. "I don't have any way to prove that, so you need to be careful when you track him down."

"You want me to track him down?" I was understandably dubious. "That doesn't sound like you. Why wouldn't you be the one to track him down and question him?"

"Because an edict came through the higher-ups last night," Augie replied. "Until Abigail declares Blair Whitney's death a murder I have nothing to investigate. I'm the chief of security, but essentially my hands are tied. There's absolutely nothing I can do about it – trust me, I put up a heckuva fight – and I'm in a pickle."

Most grown men couldn't get away with using the word

"pickle" to describe a situation like this, but I decided to let him slide. "That's why you got so drunk last night, isn't it? You were upset about being ordered off the case and because your good-guy brain couldn't simply abandon the investigation you decided to wallow."

"Pretty much. What's your excuse?"

"I'm a lush."

Augie snorted. "Cute. I don't believe it, but I guess it's something we can talk about later. For now, I can't move on Charles Whitney because I've been ordered not to. I could lose my job over this, and as much as I want to get justice for Blair Whitney, I really like my job."

I couldn't blame him. I remained suspicious about a few things, though. "Did the order to close the investigation come from Buddy?"

Augie's eyebrows winged up. "Buddy? Why would he be involved?"

I swallowed hard. The information highway was a two-way street, and he'd blessed me with important gossip so I felt I owed him the same. "Buddy and Blair Whitney went to college together. He got her discounts on procedures and she pretended to fawn all over him in exchange."

"How do you know that?"

"Mitzi."

"Mitzi confided in you?"

"She ... was motivated to share information," I hedged, suddenly uncomfortable. "You know you could get in a lot of trouble for passing on this information to me, don't you?"

Augie nodded. "Yes, but I also know that you won't let this go until you've tracked down every possibility. I don't know why you're so invested in this — I have a few ideas, but we can talk about them another time — but I know you'll figure out the truth."

"How do you know that?"

"You always do." Augie slapped his knees before standing, signifying he was about to say his goodbyes and leave. "You're smart and tenacious. I have faith you'll use those skills to do what I can't."

For some reason the simple statement touched me. "I think that's the nicest thing you've ever said to me."

"You're also idiotic and jump in with both feet without looking," Augie added. "Don't call me if you get in trouble. I can't be the one to bail you out because then everyone will know I set you on this path."

I scowled. "That charm thing you pride yourself on comes and goes at the oddest of times."

"It does," Augie agreed. "Whatever you do, be careful. Even though Abigail won't term it a murder, we both know it is. That means you could be on the trail of someone dangerous."

"Don't worry. I know how to take care of myself."

"You're also irritating enough to drive men to murder. Make sure that doesn't happen this time."

"You can count on it. I'm not ready to die for someone else's cause."

"Keep it that way."

Eleven

I remained troubled by Augie's visit even after I'd finally worked up the courage to head to town. Instead of heading to the coffee shop – which would have been my first destination on a normal day – I decided a visit to Zola was in order. I had two reasons fueling me. The first was that I wanted to get one of my witchy fights out of the way and Zola was the least likely to hold a grudge. The second was because she had access to hangover remedies in her shop.

Yes, I'm *that* witch. I'm willing to put up with a fight to get rid of a headache. I'm willing to look like a user to get what I want. I'm willing to feign I was wrong (mostly because I'm never *really* wrong) to get relief. Sue me.

Zola stood behind the counter, hands on hips, and barely looked up when I slid through the front door. I knew she was aware of my presence because I opted to park my Vespa directly in front of the store – right next to her scooter, which featured baskets for carrying plants – so there was no way she didn't see me when I pulled up. As for acknowledging me, apparently she had other plans.

"You don't have to pretend you don't see me," I announced as I sauntered down the middle aisle and made a big show of ogling her most recent offerings. "The wormwood and nightshade look great. You really outdid yourself this year."

Zola slanted her eyes until they were nothing but glittery slits. "What do you want, Skye?"

Ugh. Did she have to be so aggressive when I was nursing a hangover? "I want quite a few things, but I think my ultimate goal is world peace." I offered a cheeky grin, but Zola's lips didn't twitch, causing me to sober. So much for charming her.

"What do you really want, Skye?"

Oh, so she was going to play it that way. "I'm looking for some valerian root."

Zola remained where she was and I had the distinct impression she was imagining doing something painful to me. She needn't have bothered because I'd already done something painful to myself. And, quite frankly, nothing could hurt more than the conversation I was forced to share with Augie this morning. How much more was I expected to suffer?

"The valerian root is two weeks from being ready," Zola said after a beat. "Come back then." She turned her attention to the plant she was trimming, ignoring my presence as I prowled through the aisles.

"How can you not have valerian root?" I really needed it. My head felt as if the little monster living inside, the one who kept knocking on my skull, was about to break through and start terrorizing the world. "That's a standard. You always have it."

"Always is an absolute. I don't believe in absolutes."

"Oh, geez." I rolled my eyes and focused on the nearest green sprout. "What about some calamus root?"

"Nope."

That figured. "Corydalis?"

Zola shook her head.

"White willow?"

"Nuh-uh."

"Skullcap?"

"You're fresh out of luck."

Something very odd was going on here. "Are you really out of those things or just out of them for me?"

Zola beamed as she lifted her eyes. "What do you think?"

I dragged a restless hand through my hair and closed the distance to the counter. "I think you're ticked about what happened last night. To be fair, it wasn't my fault. It was an accident."

"You accidentally dosed us with truth serum?" Zola didn't look convinced. "That seems unlikely. You know what truth serum does to us. We're not genetically human, so giving us magically enhanced serum that's geared toward humans is a recipe for disaster."

Oh, I hate it when she gets condescending. "I didn't mean for you guys to drink it. I certainly didn't mean for me to drink it. I mixed the rum runners and left them on the bar for two seconds so I could talk to Dylan. Bonnie thought I was mixing them for the four of us and delivered them to you. How can that possibly be blamed on me?"

Zola shot me a withering look. "Do you really want me to answer that?"

I wasn't sure. "I didn't plan it. I ended up more embarrassed than anybody else anyway, so I don't see why you have your witch hazel in a twist."

"I sang 'Like a Virgin.'"

Whoops. I forgot about that. "And you have a lovely singing voice. I know you touched me for the very first time."

Zola glared. "If you think I'm helping you after what you pulled last night ... ."

"The truth serum was for Lena and Rebecca. I added the daughter and assistant for good measure. I wasn't aiming for you, for crying out loud."

"Why were you even aiming for them?"

The question caught me off guard. "What do you mean?"

"I mean ... why were you trying to get the truth out of them?" Zola persisted. "You're not the type who generally sticks her neck out to root out someone else's truth. But you're fixated on doing exactly that. Why?"

She was so not going to turn this into some sort of psychiatry session with Dr. Zola sitting in a chair while I stretched out on a couch and spilled my feelings. "I have no idea what you're talking about."

"You know exactly what I'm talking about," Zola snapped. "You're fixated on Blair Whitney, although for the life of me I can't figure out why. You didn't even know her."

"No," I agreed.

"So ... what's the deal?"

"It doesn't matter." I was too tired to continue the discussion and let loose a long-suffering sigh as I turned to leave. "Thanks for all your lovely help."

"I'll loan you some of my valerian root if you answer the question," Zola offered, causing me to freeze and slowly turn back.

"You said you didn't have any valerian root."

"No, I said I didn't have any valerian root for sale," Zola corrected. "That doesn't mean I don't have any for personal use."

That was so ... Zola, the master manipulator. "And all you want in exchange for the valerian root is what?"

"An honest answer." Zola folded her arms over her chest. The look she lobbed in my direction was weighted. "Why are you so obsessed with figuring out what happened to Blair Whitney?"

It was an easy question and it should've had an easy answer. I held my hands palms out and shrugged. "I don't know." That wasn't entirely a lie. "I feel it's important to find out who killed her. There's something inside propelling me to do it."

"And you obviously think it was the mistress?"

Did I? Augie's bombshell offered up another tantalizing option. "What would you say if I told you that Blair Whitney's husband arrived on the island the day she died?" I sidled back to the counter and ran my fingers over the velvety stem of the plant Zola toiled over.

"I would say I don't understand."

"It's true. Charles Whitney is at the Beachcomber Resort. He checked in about twelve hours before his wife died and a good twenty-two hours before I tripped over her body."

Instead of offering up a snarky observation, Zola looked thoughtful. "That's weird, right?"

I was relieved that she agreed. "I tend to believe that's really weird. The thing is, I thought the mistress was the obvious choice – I mean, who brings their husband's mistress on vacation with them? But what if the husband came to town under the radar so he could kill his wife and then pop out of town before anyone realized he was even here?"

"I would say there're several problems with your theory," Zola replied without hesitation. "The first is that you can't get a hotel room on this island without a credit card. It's simply impossible in this day and age. That means there has to be a record of Charles Whitney staying at the hotel."

"Unless he used a friend's credit card ... or a corporate account card."

"I guess that's fair," Zola offered after a moment. "That doesn't change the fact that if he murdered her and didn't want people to know he was here he wouldn't have checked into a hotel at all. Plus, well, wouldn't he have taken off directly after the deed?"

"Maybe, unless for some reason he thought it was better to lay low."

"Let's say that's true. Why stay several days after? That's just begging for trouble."

Huh. She wasn't wrong. "Then why not make his presence known? Why go through all the subterfuge?"

"I don't know. How did you even find out about this?"

"Augie." His name was out of my mouth before I thought better about sharing the information. "I mean ... don't tell anyone." I lowered my voice when Zola's eyes lit with mirth. "I'm serious. He could lose his job over the information he slipped me, and that doesn't seem fair because he was trying to help."

"Since when are you and Augie so tight?" Zola drawled. "I mean ... I don't remember you guys sharing information before."

"His hands are tied. He can't investigate unless Abigail deems it a homicide, which she hasn't yet. He could lose his job over this. He's been ordered to ignore whatever evidence he finds. He's upset."

Zola sobered. "I actually can see Augie being upset. He's a good guy and always tries to do the right thing."

"You make him sound like a martyr."

"He's pretty close."

"Don't ever tell him that. His head will only get bigger, and it's already in danger of needing its own ZIP code."

Zola tapped her bottom lip as she surveyed me with unreadable eyes. "You and Augie spent a lot of time together last night."

"Yes, and you know why. I had no idea until after it

happened that I'd downed one of the dosed drinks, and by then it was too late. You know what those drinks do to us."

"I do." Zola nodded. "They make us stupid and slow. I know if you fight them the magic overflows into something else. I watched you last night, so I know that your excess magic oozed out in the form of flirting."

I was pretty sure I hated the way she phrased that. "Nothing oozed out."

"You two danced ... a lot." Zola, lost in her own little world, barely looked at me. "You drank ... a lot. You also laughed ... a lot. You were all over each other the entire night."

"That was the spell. It made me act out of sorts."

"That was partially the spell, and it didn't make you do anything you weren't willing to do," Zola corrected. "You know that's not how magic works."

Ugh. This was a conversational rabbit hole I didn't want to go down. It didn't look as if I had a choice, though. "And what are you suggesting?"

"That you spent a lot of time with Augie last night." Zola's grin was impish. "I was distracted by a few things of my own, but when I did see you, I believe you were having a good time."

Well, great. This was the last conversation I wanted to have with a pounding head and a mounting to-do list. "Listen here ... ."

Zola barreled forward. "Not only were you two together last night, now you've suddenly shown up with information that came from Augie. Did he give you this information last night? Because, and I'm going to be honest here, I don't think he was sober enough to deliver any believable information."

She wasn't wrong. "He didn't deliver it last night."

"I see."

"He told me the story this morning."

Zola's lips curved in such a fashion I wanted to smack her face to get the smirk to disappear. "You saw him last night and this morning, huh? Is there something you want to tell me?"

"Yes. You're being a busybody ... and being ridiculous to boot. There's nothing going on between Augie and me, so get your mind out of the gutter."

"Uh-huh." Zola was obviously dubious. "Why did he show up at your house this morning? Curious minds want to know."

"Because he wanted to apologize for last night." I could've lied — actually, I thought about it — but it seemed a wasted effort. "He blamed himself for the flirting. He didn't realize I was causing it and felt terrible."

"Oh." Zola sobered. "That's nowhere near as fun of a story as I thought it would be. Poor Augie."

"Yeah, well, I'm not sure I'm willing to take it that far," I grumbled. "He had the information about Charles Whitney yesterday. Someone anonymously slipped it under his office door, which is weird in itself, and then he was ordered to back off the investigation."

"Which explains why he got that drunk in the first place," Zola mused. "I wondered. He's not a huge drinker. I mean, he likes to have a good time and all, but he's not the type to get witch-faced for nothing."

"No, and he felt like a gigantic creeper this morning and brought me coffee and an apology. As part of that, he gave me the information about Charles Whitney. He thought I could investigate him without getting into trouble. I won't be in danger of losing my job for following the information, so ... ."

"So you're going to follow the information," Zola finished.

"I am." I bobbed my head. "I know you don't understand why I want answers. I'm not sure I really do either. I only know I tripped over Blair Whitney and now I feel responsible for finding out how she died, *why* she died."

Zola blinked several times in rapid succession and then exhaled heavily. "Fine. I guess I understand, although not really. You're doing what you have to do."

"Exactly. I need valerian root to do it."

"I'll get some from the back," Zola mumbled to herself as she disappeared into the back room, allowing me a few minutes to peruse the plants ... and change the small signs to misidentify everything, because even though I was grateful for the imminent headache relief, I was still me and wanted to mess with her. I was back at the counter by the time Zola returned.

"Don't overdo it." She dropped four small nubs in my hand. "I would put it in a tea to get it to work faster."

"I was going to chew it."

Zola arched an eyebrow. "That sounds ... classy."

I smirked. "Thanks for this." I cupped my hand around the roots. "I'll let you know if I come up with any good information regarding Charles Whitney."

"Just be careful," Zola ordered. "If you're right, he could be a murderer. If he catches you sneaking around, he won't like it."

I snickered. "You sound like Augie."

"Augie wanted you to be careful?"

"He was adamant about it."

"Yeah." Zola adopted a knowing look. "I think Augie is right. You should definitely be careful ... and watch your back."

"Trust me. Charles Whitney won't get a chance to sneak up on me. I don't need to watch my back."

"I was talking about watching your back with Kenna," Zola clarified. "After what happened last night, she's on the warpath. When she finds you it won't be pretty."

I swallowed hard. Yup. I should've been expecting that. "I'm not afraid of her." I was more bravado than brains sometimes. "She can come find me whenever she wants."

"I'll tell her you said that."

"Great. I think that will be just ... great."

That was so not great.

Twelve

I spent what was left of the morning (which wasn't much) watching room sixteen at the Beachcomber Resort. Because of the facility's layout, each room had a private entrance. That meant I had to sit on the beach, pretending the already bright sun didn't exacerbate my pounding headache, and chew on valerian root.

Charles Whitney didn't as much as stir. That meant I needed to come up with another plan.

Once my hangover started to ease, I took advantage of the hotel's dining room accommodations and slipped inside. I didn't recognize the young woman behind the desk at first glance, so I decided to bypass her in case I needed to run a scam later. I grabbed a table in the small dining room. The waitress who hit me up there three minutes later was a familiar face.

Faye Bradshaw was the friendly sort. She was in her thirties, a single mother, and she worked three jobs to keep her two kids in nice clothes. She wasn't a complainer by nature — something I didn't understand, because if I had two kids and had been abandoned by my husband who took off to play hide the seashell with a girl barely out of high school I'd totally be bitter – and she graced me with a bright smile.

"This is a surprise." Faye was simply too likable to be rude to, so I grinned back. "What's the special occasion?"

I shrugged, noncommittal. "Does there have to be a special occasion for me to stop in for lunch?"

"Honey, the chicken wraps are good, but they're hardly worth a trip across town."

She had a point. "Speaking of that, I want a chicken wrap with ranch, fries and an iced tea."

"Sure." Faye jotted down the order. "Are you going to tell me why you're really here?"

"No. I'm on a mission."

"That sounds like you." Faye snickered as she started to move away from the table. "I'll be back in a minute with your drink. I'll tell Kenna you're here so she can join you as soon as she's done in the lobby."

It was an offhand comment, but it made the hair on the back of my neck stand up and threaten revolt. "I'm sorry."

"Kenna," Faye repeated. "She's in the lobby. We have a new desk clerk and Kenna is taking photos for that quarterly newsletter she prints to play up new faces in Eternal Springs."

Ah, yes, the newsletter that anyone with taste uses to line their birdcages. What were the freaking odds that Kenna would be here doing that today? They had to be astronomical. "Oh, well ... ." I swallowed hard. "If Kenna is busy you don't have to tell her I'm here. I don't want to interrupt her very important newsletter work. It might throw off her entire day if she knows I'm here."

"I don't think that's true." Faye winked. "I'm sure she'll be happy to have someone to eat with. I'll tell her."

"I ... ." Faye was already gone before I could think up a way to stop her from alerting Kenna to my presence. That left me with nothing to do but wait until Kenna appeared in the doorway between the lobby and dining room.

I saw her first. She wore one of her color-coordinated suits and a pair of shoes that I was certain cost more than my Vespa. She scanned the room and by the time her gaze landed on me I was a ball of nerves.

"Here we go," I muttered under my breath as she squared her shoulders and headed in my direction.

"Well, well, well. Look who we have here." Kenna sounded like the cat who was about to eat the bat. "I'm surprised you're out and about so early after your little show with Augie last night."

I scowled. "If you have something to say, please don't hold back on my account."

"I don't intend to." Kenna plopped herself into the one seat she knew would cut off my avenue of escape should I decide to run. "I blame you for last night. I hope you know that."

Who else would she blame? No, really. Who? I accidentally caused the town to think she was a drunken *American Idol* wannabe. There was no one else to blame. "Oh, come on. It wasn't that bad. I personally think everyone loved your rendition of 'Man, I Feel Like a Woman.' Dylan even asked if you were really a man pretending to be a woman."

The only thing keeping Kenna from leaping across the table and strangling me was her insistence that the community see her as a professional. "Do you think that's funny?"

"I think there's a lot that's not funny happening on this island right now, so I have to get my laughs where I can," I replied without hesitation. "I'm sorry about what happened last night. No, I really am. I can't go back in time and change it, so I'm not certain what you want from me."

My matter-of-fact statement caught Kenna off guard. "Why are you acting so strange today? In fact, why are you even here? It would behoove you to lay low and hide for the next few days. That way people might forget the way you and Augie practically rubbed yourselves against one another for three hours straight."

Now she was hitting below the broom. "I did not rub myself against him." Okay, maybe a little, but I was very careful to make sure no one saw when I did it. "What happened last night was a fluke, so there's no reason to dwell on it ... even though I know you totally will because that's your way."

"Did you tell Augie it was a fluke?" Kenna challenged. "I'm not sure he'd agree."

"Oh, he agrees. We already talked about it."

"You did?"

"Yes."

"And what did he say?"

"He blamed himself, which makes me feel even worse than I already do," I admitted. "He thought he did something inappropriate and was horrified."

"Oh." Kenna leaned back in her chair. "Actually, that shouldn't surprise me. That's how he is. I guess it makes sense for him to assume he did something wrong."

"Don't worry. I made sure he was back to his obnoxious self before sending him on his way this morning. He's over it."

"Are you over it?"

What was that supposed to mean? "I was never under it ... or him ... or you know what I mean. Stop grinning like a loon. It makes you look deranged, and that's going to ruin that professional image you've worked so hard to cultivate even though no one but you cares."

Kenna's smile slipped. "There's nothing wrong with being professional."

"Of course not."

"You should try it."

"I'll keep that in mind."

The anger flowing between us ratcheted up a notch. We were often the first to fly off the handle when it came to disagreements.

"If that's all you have to say to me, I came here for a quiet lunch and alone time," I said. "Sharing conversation over lunch will eliminate that possibility for both of us."

"I don't want to eat with you any more than you want to eat with me," Kenna sneered, standing. "I hope you have a nice lunch ... and don't choke on it more than once or twice."

I should've left the situation alone. She was furious and ready to strike, and I was agitated and poised to annoy. It was a combustible mixture.

The problem is, even when I know I should let things play out in a calm manner I often can't stop myself from doing the opposite. This was one of those times.

"By the way, I hear your rendition of 'Livin' la Vida Loca' was everyone's favorite last night," I offered. "The way you shook your bonbon was a particular treat."

That did it. I knew I'd gone a step too far even before I smelled smoke. It was too late to pull the comment back. Kenna vented her frustration on a nearby plant, which burst into flames. It was such a large explosion that the smoke alarm immediately started whining, at which point the guests and workers began panicking.

"Omigod! The hotel is on fire!"

And just like that, I had the diversion I was looking to create. I guess things work out as they're supposed to at least a time or two.

I MANAGED TO ESCAPE from Kenna's wrath by using my beauty and brains. Okay, I waited until she was distracted and ran like a scared little girl. What? She can start fires with her mind. I've seen, like, five movies based on that exact scenario and not one of them turns out well.

I was at the back of the hotel when Charles Whitney's door opened and he stepped out. He seemed confused – I didn't blame him – and he looked in both directions before shrugging and starting toward me. He hadn't seen me yet, which was a good thing, because I had a plan.

I pressed my hands to my forehead, whispered the glamour spell, and smoothed the front of my shirt as I slid around the building. I timed it exactly right so Charles would inadvertently run into me ... literally.

"Oomph." I bounced off him, making a big show of grunting as I started falling back. I expected him to grab my shoulders to keep me from falling, but the look he gave me was one of annoyance instead of sympathy when I hit the floor.

"What are you doing here, Rebecca?"

He didn't look happy to see his mistress. In fact, he looked downright furious. That was interesting. "I came to see you." That seemed a reasonable answer. I hadn't spent any time with Rebecca, so I wasn't familiar with her mannerisms, but I was hopeful that wouldn't be too much of an issue if I limited my time with Charles.

"Why would you possibly come to see me?" Charles' tone was biting.

"Because I love you." The words burned coming out – he was a gross old man sleeping with his daughter's best friend, after all – but I somehow managed to maintain my cover. "You're my ... snuggly bear."

The look Charles shot me as I struggled to my feet and dusted off my sore rear end said I'd taken it too far. I wasn't surprised. I often take things too far. Go figure. "What did you just call me?"

"I was trying to be flirty." I decided to go on the offensive to confuse him. "Don't worry. It won't happen again. I'm sure my imagination won't allow it."

"Whatever." Charles rubbed his elbow as he glared. "You still haven't answered my question. Why are you here?"

"I wanted to see you. I thought we should talk."

"What exactly do you think we should talk about, Rebecca? What does that puny brain of yours need explained this time?"

My mouth dropped open at his hurtful words and tone. "Seriously?"

"I told you yesterday that we can't be seen together on this island!" Charles barked. "I wasn't talking merely to hear myself talk when I said it. I was serious."

Clearly he was serious a hundred percent of the time. I should've realized he wasn't the sort of guy who was in it for the laughs. "Yeah, well ... you're not the boss of me."

"I'm not the boss of you?" Charles' eyes widened to comical proportions. "That's exactly what I am. Who pays for that condo you love so much? Who gives you a weekly allowance? Who made sure you got the stupid limited edition purple color for the BMW you wanted? That was me."

"Those were ... gifts." I felt as if I was behind in the conversation and had no hope of catching up. "You said those were gifts."

"No, I told you what I expected in return," Charles corrected, his lecherous gaze causing my skin to crawl. "I spelled out what was expected of both of us when we started this, Rebecca."

"I ... ." What was going on here?

"You what?" Charles' face was red with fury. "You forgot? You always forget. I shouldn't always have to remind you."

He looked so angry I momentarily worried about my safety. Then I remembered I was a witch and he was an angry old man who very likely needed to pop Viagra to get his motor running. "Knock it off." I slapped a hand in the middle of his chest to make sure he didn't advance. "There's no reason to get worked up. You're old. Your heart probably can't take the workout."

Charles' face twisted. "What did you say?"

"You heard me." I extended a finger when he opened his mouth to say something that was sure to be hateful and vitriolic. "Don't even think of yelling at me ... or doing whatever it is you usually do. I'm not in the mood and I have limited time."

Charles was flabbergasted. "So what are you doing here?"

"I want to know how long you plan to stay."

"I already told you that I can't leave right now." Charles' temper was on full display. "Are you stupid? Do you listen?" He rapped his knuckles against the side of my head, causing my temper to spurt. "If I leave now it will look like I'm running. That's not good, you moron. I have to stay here now. I have to deal with Blair's death. I have to pretend to be the good and caring husband, even though I only came to this island to make sure Blair didn't kill you and leave your body in the woods for the scavengers to fight over. Do you have any idea how annoying it is to pretend to be someone I'm not?"

"I know how annoying you are," I shot back.

"What?"

"If you ever do that again I will hurt you." I mimed cracking my own head with my fist so he would know what I was talking about. "I'm a master at inflicting pain, too. Just try it."

Charles' face flooded with confusion. "Why are you acting like this? Are you drunk? It's barely noon and you're drinking. That's great."

"I haven't been drinking." Now I kind of wished I had a

rum runner, though. Hangover be damned. "Are you always like this?"

"Like what?"

I didn't have time to play this game. Plus, I was coming dangerously close to blowing my cover. Clearly the real Rebecca didn't have a problem with Charles' attitude. I felt sorry for her ... and kind of wanted to shake her until she came to her senses.

"What's your next plan of attack?" I asked, forcing myself to remain on task. "What are you going to do about Blair now that she's ... out of the picture?"

"I haven't decided yet."

"What are you going to do about me?"

Charles furrowed his brow. "What do you mean by that?"

"I want to know what the future holds. I want to know if we're going to get married. I want to know if we're going to move in together. I want to know how long we have to wait to go public. Those things are important to me. I don't really care what's important to you."

Charles worked his jaw, but no sound came out. He was silent for so long I thought I'd inadvertently broken him. When he finally did speak, it was with a tone laced with venom and hatred. "Are you trying to kill me?"

Was that a rhetorical question? "No, but I haven't ruled it out."

"None of that will ever happen. I told you from the start this was going nowhere. Are you telling me you thought that was going to change simply because Blair happened to take a rock to the head? I'm not going to change my mind."

None of this made sense. None of it. Charles' words were pretty much the exact opposite of Lena's. Either someone was lying or he or she didn't understand the realities of the conversation.

"So ... nothing is going to happen?"

"Exactly." Charles poked his finger into my breastbone. "Now you need to get out of here. No one can see us together. I told you that yesterday when you showed up in that expensive outfit you wanted to put on my credit card."

I stared at him for a long moment, unblinking. Then I did the only thing I could do and rammed my knee into his groin. "I'm leaving. Try not to miss me too much while I'm gone."

Charles sputtered as he listed to the side, his face a mottled shade of red as foam appeared at the corners of his mouth. I was already facing the opposite direction when I heard him hit the floor. If Charles Whitney wanted to convince me he wasn't responsible for his wife's death, he had a long way to go. The problem was, Rebecca couldn't be removed from the list either. She clearly had her own set of issues.

What the heck was going on in this little group of rabid crazies?

Thirteen

I was so infuriated by my interaction with Charles Whitney that I needed to blow off steam. For me, that meant taking a long ride on my Vespa. The island is only so big — at least the parts I deign to visit — so that essentially meant I drove around for an hour and then headed to the newspaper office, still fuming.

The Town Croaker was essentially a three-person operation, but I did most of the heavy lifting. I had an occasional layout person and an advertising person, and they both worked from home. I was the only one who ever visited the office regularly, and I was seriously starting to wonder if it was a waste to keep up the lease.

Of course, my ultimate problem was that I didn't want to operate The Town Croaker out of my home and the building's true merit came in the form of a space to hide when I needed a break from Swoops and his corned beef hash mania. Also, well, who doesn't like having his or her own building from which to conduct business?

I parked the Vespa in front of the building, leaving my helmet hanging from the handlebar as I scuffed my feet against the sidewalk and trudged toward the front door. I had my key out and my mind on running a background check on Charles Whitney when a foul odor – one that would make rancid eggs stand up and point – assailed my senses.

I stopped in my tracks, my mind working overtime. I first thought someone dumped a body on the property and it had been left to rot. Yes, I'm morbid like that. I watch a lot of horror movies, so a dead body is often my initial guess.

It didn't take me long to realize that was probably not the case, especially because I'd stopped at the building the previous day on my way to Coconuts and the smell hadn't been present.

I turned slowly, opening my senses and allowing my magic to seep out and form a net of sorts. I used it like a grid, carefully scanning each direction. I didn't ultimately sense danger as I slowly twirled, but I did feel ... something.

Was it eyes?

I had trouble believing anything could sneak that close without activating my inner danger alarm.

Was it a malevolent force?

Maybe. After the fall of the school we remained behind for a reason. We were distracted, and that allowed a door that should have always remained closed to blow open. Even now, the ramifications of that one act haunted us. It was why we couldn't leave. More importantly, it was why we couldn't talk about it.

Things shifted into place quickly when I spied the ancient wishing well at the front of the property. I strode in that direction, determined despite the smell, and frowned as I leaned over and peered inside.

In horror movies the audience often understands what's about to happen. Movie watchers scream at the hapless heroine.

Don't go in there.

Don't look in the closet.
Don't go upstairs.
Don't sleep with him.

The heroine almost always does those things and somehow she survives. That was me today, because even as I held up my keychain and flicked the switch on the small attached flashlight my brain told me I was making a mistake. It wasn't until I saw the scaly creature sitting at the bottom of the well, his black eyes large and soulful, that I realized exactly how big a mistake I had made.

"Oh, geez!"

The creature – a mix between what looked to be a bad gremlin and a stoned Godzilla wannabe with pink claws – didn't appear afraid as he stared back. He sat in the filthy water, which had somehow turned green, and let loose a loud belch.

"Oh, great." I jerked up my head and glanced around, making sure I remained alone before speaking. When I glanced back down I found the creature had shifted so he was leaning back and I could see his ... for the love of the Goddess, please tell me that's a tail! I slapped my hand over my eyes and did my best not to panic. "Why are you here?"

I didn't know if the creature would answer. In truth, I wasn't sure it could answer. Not everything that crawls through the door has vocal cords. Thankfully for me – or maybe, upon further reflection it wasn't something to be thankful for at all – this creature had the gift of conversation.

"Hello there, sugar."

Oh, I wanted to find a hole – a different hole, mind you – and crawl inside. This is not how I envisioned spending my day. "What are you?"

The creature raised a slimy green hand and held it palm up. "What are you?"

"I'm an ... Aquarian."

"That means you're headstrong, sarcastic, temperamental and sometimes aloof."

Hmm. I didn't expect him to know anything about astrology. "Sure. And what are you?"

"I'm a Scorpio."

I waited for him to continue.

"That means I'm focused, brave, jealous and a little manipulative."

Oh, for the love of all that's witchy. "That's fascinating and it makes me want to buy a book on astrology." That was a total lie. "I'm more interested in *what* you are. Like ... I'm a human. What are you?"

"You're not human."

"I am so."

"You are not." My new friend made a face. "You're a witch. You're one of the ones from the school, the gate watchers. Apparently you're not doing your job, because I walked right through the gate."

I narrowed my eyes. Could that be true? Did the gate somehow blow open a second time? I instantly tossed out the notion. If the gate were fully open, we would be dealing with a lot worse than stinky lizard monsters in the wishing well. No, he was another escapee. He made a hole, crawled through it, and it was my job to put him back.

Too bad I had other things on my mind.

"How long have you been here?"

"Oh, not long." The creature splashed in the water, making the smell double ... and momentarily remind me of waterlogged cheese left out in the sun for too long. "I'm thinking about making this my new home. What do you think?"

"No."

"I know it doesn't look like much, but if I knock out a wall and dig a bit ... I think it will be quite posh."

"Absolutely not." I was firm. "You can't stay here." And by that, I meant he couldn't stay on this side of the gate. It was probably best not to bring that up right now, though. "You have to find someplace else. If the locals see you ... ."

"I know I look a bit different, but I have a lovely personality."

"You smell like athlete's foot mixed with rotten cottage cheese."

The creature smiled, showing off a row of razor sharp teeth that made me think taking him down wasn't exactly going to be easy. "That's my signature fragrance. I'm thinking of selling it to fund my well renovations."

Oh, now he was just messing with me. "Listen ... scaly thing ... you can't stay here. I have no idea when you decided to move in – or why, for that matter – but you can't stay here."

"My name is Odactortim."

"What's an Odactortim?"

"That's my name."

"I'm just going to call you Tim."

"Laziness is ugly."

"I'm fine with that." There was no way I was going to debate my personality flaws with a scaled creature who wanted to expand my wishing well so he could live in it. "You can't stay in here. I mean ... you have to stay until dark because if someone sees you wandering around it will create a panic. After that, you've got to ... you know ... vamoose."

"I don't believe I'm going to agree to your terms." The creature's smile was back. "I'm happy here and there's nothing you can do to force me out of my new digs. I mean ... absolutely nothing."

We'd have to see about that. For now, I had no choice but to let him be. I couldn't very well engage in a magical battle when someone could walk or drive by at any moment. I would have to come back to force a relocation after dark.

"Just don't get into trouble. And try to do something about that smell," I ordered, taking a step away from the well. Something occurred to me before I could leave, and I peered over the edge again. "What do you eat, by the way?"

"Are you asking me to dinner?"

"Not last time I checked. You don't eat people, do you?"

Tim made a face. "Of course not! Who would eat people? That's absolutely disgusting."

"Great." Whew! That was a relief. One less thing to worry about.

"I eat babies. They're much more tender. They're delicious with barbecue sauce and cooked over an open fire. I'm looking forward to sampling the local cuisine starting tonight."

Son of a ... ! I totally should've seen that coming.

"Don't even think about it," I warned, extending a finger. "You're not allowed to eat babies."

"We shall see." Tim closed his eyes and sighed as he tried to get comfortable. "Now, if you'll excuse me, it's my nap time. You're ruining the vibe of my new place. Next time you want to stop by, bring a housewarming gift."

The next time I dropped by I was going to bring a sword and magical trap. "Don't get too comfortable."

Tim was already softly snoring.

IT WASN'T EXACTLY EASY to concentrate on computer work when I had a baby-eating lizard monster living in my wishing well, but I'd managed to push Tim out of my mind long enough to Google Charles Whitney. What I found wasn't exactly the stuff of fluffy dreams and cloud dancing.

Charles Whitney was considered a shark in the business world and a paragon of virtue in his private life. I couldn't find any gossipy whisperings about his mistress, who happened to be the same age as his daughter and apparently five apples short of a pie.

He was a broker, although I didn't know everything that entailed, and his claim to fame was making his clients extremely rich while helping them dodge taxes. No, seriously, that was all out there for public perusal and apparently he was proud of it.

I didn't know what to make of it.

I was so lost in my research that I didn't hear the front door open or notice the shadowy figure was almost on top of me before my senses kicked in and I lashed out with my foot to kick whatever it was – perhaps Tim decided I looked as tasty as a baby – in the knee with enough force to cause the interloper to cry out and drop to the ground with a loud thud and whimper.

Unfortunately for me, my new visitor wasn't Tim but Augie. "What are you doing?"

I hopped to my feet and grabbed his elbow as he grunted and tried to straighten. My kick was straight and true, and he was probably lucky I had a bad angle or we would be waiting for the ambulance cart about now. "Have you ever heard of knocking?"

I helped Augie to a chair and knelt so I could look at his knee. He was wearing jeans, so that wasn't an easy task. Without thinking, I started at his ankles and slid my hands under his jeans. I didn't notice how inappropriate I was being until he squirmed when my hands hit his calves.

"Knock that off!" Augie barked, causing me to jerk back.

"I was trying to see if I broke anything." I slowly withdrew my hands, hating the way my cheeks flushed as I fought to gain control of my senses. His skin shouldn't have been that smooth ... or hot. Sure, he had hairy legs, but he was a dude. That was expected. "I wasn't trying to feel you up or anything."

"I didn't say you were trying to feel me up." Augie looked as uncomfortable as I felt. "I just ... I'm ticklish."

"Good to know." I blew out a sigh as I found the courage to meet his gaze. "Are you in pain?"

"I'm with you, aren't I? That typically means I'm in pain."

I pursed my lips. "I was asking if I should call for the ambulance."

Augie made a face. "Absolutely not. That will totally ruin my street cred."

"You're a rent-a-cop at a resort that caters to plastic surgery addicts. You don't have any street cred."

"Says you," Augie shot back, his temper flaring even as the blush I caused to flood his cheeks when I reached into his pants fled. "I'll have you know that everyone in town thinks I'm a total badass."

"Uh-huh." That was the most ludicrous thing I'd ever heard and only an hour before I'd been having a discussion with a lizard creature that had taken up residence in a wishing well. "I'm sure everyone trembles in fear when you're around."

"They do."

"I just said that." I slowly made my way around to the opposite side of my desk and smoothed my hair as I sat. "So ... um ... what are you doing here?"

"Being a badass."

I couldn't hide my smile. "Other than that."

"Checking on you," Augie answered without hesitation. "I wanted to make sure you didn't get into any trouble when you decided to track down Charles Whitney. I heard the Beachcomber Resort had a fire drill this afternoon and I assumed that was because of you."

"That's a horrible thing to say."

"Are you saying it wasn't because of you?"

Not directly. "I had nothing to do with the fire alarm going off," I supplied. "I was out there, but I spent most of the morning watching Charles Whitney's room from the beach." That wasn't a lie. "You can't blame the fire alarm on me." That, of course, was only half a lie.

Augie didn't look convinced, but he let it go. "Well, did you talk to him? Did he have anything good to say?"

This was a sticky situation and I wasn't sure how to respond. "I haven't talked to him." It seemed the easiest way to go. "I'm not sure how to approach him. I'm conducting research right now and then I will formulate a plan."

"Well, keep me updated for when this plan comes to fruition. As for the other thing ... ." He trailed off, leaving me confused.

"What other thing? I didn't realize there was an other thing."

"It's about the smell." Augie shifted in his chair, discomfort obvious.

"What smell? I showered today." It was only after I uttered the inane line that I realized what smell had caught his attention. Tim. The creature in the wishing well. The smell had spread beyond my front lawn, far enough that someone at the resort complained even though the building was located a good distance from the resort's property line. Crud on toast.

"I didn't say you smell," Augie said hurriedly. "You actually tend to smell nice ... like coconuts and lime." He shook his head to dislodge whatever fog he found himself in. "I'm talking about the smell outside. I think you might have a gas leak or something."

Uh-oh. The last thing I needed was Augie calling the gas company because he was worried about me. I had to turn this around. "Oh, I know what smell you're talking about."

"You do?" Augie leaned forward. "Where is it coming from? Something didn't die out there, did it?"

"It's not coming from here at all." I decided to force the issue because I didn't know what else to do. "I'm pretty sure it's coming from those mud pits to the east of the resort."

Augie made an incredulous face. "It is not. I followed the smell here."

"I think you just came here because you wanted to see me." I backtracked quickly. "I mean ... I think you came here because you wanted to get information from me."

"No, that was only part of the reason." Augie crossed his arms over his chest. "Seriously, what is that smell?"

"It's coming from the mud pits."

"No, it's coming from your property."

"The mud pits."

"Your property."

I slammed my hands on my desk and let my eyes fire. "The mud pits!"

"Ugh. I don't even know why I take the time to talk to you sometimes."

"That goes double for me."

Fourteen

I stopped by the wishing well long enough to give Tim a firm warning on my way out.

"You're starting to attract attention. I suggest moving as soon as darkness falls. The woods — far, far away from town — are always a good bet. I would get out while the getting is good."

Tim lazily flicked his forked tongue. "I can't leave my new home. I haven't even decorated yet."

Ugh. He was going to be a problem. "Fine." I huffed irritably as I scuffed my foot against the ground. "Don't say I didn't warn you. This won't end well."

"I'll invite you over for tea and finger foods once I have an opening in my schedule." Tim beamed so widely it made him look all the more evil. "Have a nice night."

"Yeah, yeah, yeah." I turned to leave and then stopped myself. "When you say 'finger foods,' you don't mean actual fingers, do you?"

"The secret is in the sauce."

I felt sick to my stomach as I buzzed along the side road

that led to my house, parking in the driveway and tilting my head to the side as I paused on the front porch. I was agitated, although not in the sense that someone had invaded my personal space and needed to be taken out. Still, it couldn't hurt to check. My safe place remained quiet, and I knew the only thing I'd have to contend with upon entering would be Swoops.

I dropped my messenger bag on the couch and frowned when I realized the panties and bras had been shifted from their previous locales into a pile in the middle of the room. It was a vast improvement from how things had looked when I'd left, but it was hardly how I wanted this to go.

"Is there a reason you couldn't have taken this upstairs?" I asked Swoops as he poked his head out from his corner hammock.

I was too tired. My blood sugar crashed hours ago. Death is imminent.

"Oh, don't start. I'm barely through the front door." I made a face. "You're not going to starve to death. In fact, you're in danger of being wider than you are tall these days. I'm starting to think you need to go on a diet."

The indignant noise Swoops issued told me exactly what he thought of that suggestion.

"I'm not kidding," I called out as I scooped up the pile of laundry and moved it to the basket sitting on the end table. I'm not the best housekeeper, so the laundry would most likely remain there until I got tired of going commando. "The last time you had a vet appointment I was told bats aren't supposed to be fat. It never happens."

I'm not a normal bat. I'm special.

"You're definitely special," I muttered under my breath. "I kind of want to send you to a special school you're just so darned ... special."

Swoops ignored the dig. *I'm not going on a diet. Diets are for quitters and I'm not a quitter.*

I didn't want to laugh. It would only encourage him, after all. I couldn't help myself, though. "We're at least going to start introducing more fruit into your diet."

Great. Blueberry pancakes.

I shook my head. "Just blueberries."

I'm open to negotiations ... as long as there's cake with my blueberries.

"We'll talk about it later." I flopped on the couch and planted my feet on the coffee table as I ran my rather long day through my head. I was so lost in thought I almost didn't notice when Tut wandered into the room and hopped on the chair across the way. Had he been a normal cat – one with fur and cute little markings – I probably wouldn't have paid him any heed. But he was hairless and freaky, so I simply glared once my heart rate returned to normal. "Who invited you in?"

"I'm not a vampire. I don't need to be invited in." Tut was blasé as he kneaded his claws into my chair. "You're late this evening. I thought perhaps you might find someplace else to sleep."

"And where would that be?" I got the distinct impression the sphinx cat was trying to force me out of my own home and I was decidedly uncomfortable with the realization.

"August Taylor's house."

The simple response was enough to throw me for a loop. "Excuse me?"

"Everyone in town is talking about your new romance." Tut purposely snagged his claws on the arm of the chair and gave them a vicious tug. "People are saying they knew it was coming and they can't figure out why it took you so long."

I was mortified. "Are people really saying that?"

"Of course. I only report things I've actually heard. I don't deal in make believe."

That was rich coming from a talking cat. "I don't understand why people would say that." My stomach flipped as I uneasily got to my feet. "Augie and I have always hated one another."

"Hate is a strong word."

"Fine. We've vehemently disliked one another."

"Which is another way of saying you have chemistry," Tut noted. "You fight because you like the little thrill it gives you. Now it seems you want to see what other kind of thrill he can give you."

Oh, well, that was enough of that. "You're wrong." I scorched the cat with a harsh look. "You have no idea what you're talking about. You're only here because you know it will drive me crazy."

"That sounds very unlikely."

"Listen, you bald little devil ... ." I didn't get a chance to finish my sentence – which was going to be mean and impressively threatening – because the wine bottle on the desk started squawking to let me know I had an incoming call. It wasn't just any call, mind you. It was from the home office. We all had an enchanted item that was cursed by our coven to serve as a means of communication in case of emergencies. I picked a bottle of wine because talking to those women made me want to drink. I thought I was being sarcastic at the time. Now I realize talking into a wine bottle simply makes me look like a drunk.

"What?" I snatched the bottle from the desk and practically barked my greeting.

"It's nice to hear your voice, too," the woman on the other end of the call drawled.

Jadis Beasley – or Jadis the Beastly as I liked to cackle behind her back – was my mentor. If that sounds a bit trite, I'm right there with you. Still, when I first arrived at St. Joan of Arc's school I was shuttled directly into Jadis' office. There she informed me that I was to report to her and only to her. That included times when I had gossip about the other mentors, if I happened to stumble across any while minding my own business, of course. In return she would teach me how to use magic the right way.

Now, thirteen years after the school had closed, I still found myself having to answer to the woman, even though I hated her more now than I did then.

"Jadis." I managed to keep disdain out of my voice, but just barely. "I can't tell you how happy I am to hear your voice. I was just thinking about you and it made my heart sing." I was the queen of laying it on too thick, but I was so used to it I barely noticed any longer.

"Cut the crap, Skye." Jadis was her usual perky self. "We need to talk about how you've been spending your days ... and nights."

Uh-oh. Someone had clearly been bending her ear. I shot a suspicious look to Tut, but he appeared to be asleep, his whiskers fluttering as he exhaled evenly. "I'm not sure what you're talking about," I hedged. "I've been doing the same things I always do."

"And that's only part of the problem," Jadis said. "If you were doing what you usually do I would do what I usually do."

"Which is?"

"Curse your name and the day you came into my life, and then disappear into some naked fire dancing and wine drinking."

That didn't sound so bad. "So do that. You don't have to worry about me."

"Apparently I do if the calls we've been getting are to be believed," Jadis countered.

I should've known. My witchy sisters had sold me out.

The bunch of tattletales were such babies they couldn't wait to get me in trouble with Jadis. Oh, I couldn't wait to show them exactly what I thought about their efforts. "Whatever you've heard is a vicious lie." It's always good to go on the offensive when you're being accused of something, so that's exactly what I did. "I demand proof of my misdeeds before I'll capitulate to anything."

Instead of being angry, Jadis blew out a weary sigh. "You're never going to grow up, are you?"

That was a loaded question. "I believe I'm very mature."

"Really? What's the most mature thing you did today?"

That was a good question. "I used a glamour to interrogate a potential murderer."

"And that right there is the core of our problem."

I didn't realize I'd waltzed into her well-laid trap until it was too late. This was so typical. "I'm sure I don't know what you mean."

"You are a child who never grew up despite all the lessons you should've learned. By the way, I never wanted a child."

"So why do you insist on calling to yell at me?"

"I'm not going to yell at you." I could practically picture Jadis practicing her breathing regimen to keep from exploding on the other end of the call. "I've decided that's counterproductive. You can claim I'm being mean and discount everything I say when I yell."

"I don't discount everything you say."

"How often do you listen to anything I say?"

There was no way I was going to answer that. "I'm bad at math. I would need a calculator to tally an answer and I have no idea where mine is right now. I'll try to remember to figure it later and send you a report."

"That sounds lovely," Jadis drawled. "I can't wait to read it."

And she thought I was the sarcastic one. "So ... is that everything?"

"Not even close." Jadis turned somber. "I want to talk to you about your actions since finding the body at the resort. You seem to be distracted, and that's something we can't have."

"I'm not distracted."

"So you're not spending all your time tracking down information on this dead woman?"

"Of course not."

"That means you haven't been using glamours to disguise yourself to question family members? You didn't go through the trouble of brewing truth serum that was accidentally ingested by your sister witches?"

Yup. Someone had definitely been flapping his or her lips. The question was: Was it the cat or a witchy rat?

"I'm not sure I understand the question," I replied after a beat. "I've been doing what I normally do, which is putting the welfare of the community first and running a newspaper second."

"You're a master at deflection, Skye, but I happen to know that you've been up to no good, and lying about it won't help the situation," Jadis argued. "I know all about the truth serum incident last night."

This could be a trick. It wouldn't be the first time Jadis pretended to know something to force me to confess to misdeeds she didn't have the full dirt on. "And what is it that you think you know?"

"I know you dosed Kenna, Evian, and Zola with truth serum and they made fools of themselves at karaoke."

"Well ... ."

She didn't give me a chance to shift topics. "I also know that you made something of an idiot of yourself. I believe you were all over a young man and are now the talk of the town, something we really don't want if we're going to fly under the radar."

I had no idea which witch squawked, but I was going to make all of them pay. I wasn't sure how, but my retribution would be fast and furious ... and mean and vindictive ... and itchy and scratchy ... and whatever other horrible combinations I could come up with between now and then.

"First, I maintain that Kenna, Evian, and Zola would've made fools of themselves regardless," I started. "They're very good at it. You might even say they're overachievers. As for what happened to me, I will admit I might have gotten a little ... flirty ... with one of the residents. I've known him for a long time, though, and we already talked about the issue this morning. We both agreed it was embarrassing and would never happen again."

"You really talked to him already?" Jadis sounded impressed. "That doesn't sound like you."

"We talked about it because we were both uncomfortable. We blamed it on the alcohol and have already moved on. There's nothing to worry about."

"I'm not worried about you getting involved with August Taylor," Jadis said. "I'm worried about you outing our secret. You need to be more careful with your magic. If the locals were to ever find out what you really are – what we all really are – I'm afraid the fallout would lead to the downfall of Eternal Springs. They have no idea what they're up against if the four of you are forced to leave, and I can see them trying to evict you if they ever found out what you are."

I could see that, too. It was a terrifying thought.

"You don't have to worry about that." I shook myself out of my melancholy. "They won't find out. I made an error last night. I'll admit that. It won't happen again."

"So you're going to give up your investigation into this woman's death?"

Oh, I didn't say that. "I'm going to focus on my work."

Jadis made a clucking sound with her tongue. "I know what that means. That's a sly way for you to say you're going to do what you want and there's nothing I can do to stop you."

She wasn't wrong. "How is life on the mainland?"

"Oh, don't go there." Jadis sucked in a breath and I knew she was working overtime to calm herself. "You need to make sure that you keep your priorities in order. I'm not saying a murder isn't something to be concerned about, but there are plenty of people on that island who can solve a murder. What you need to do ... well, only your sister witches and you can do that. It's important to remember that."

It wasn't as if I were in a position to forget. Speaking of that, ... "Have you ever seen a green lizard creature that stinks to high heaven and wants to live in a few feet of water? He claims he eats babies."

Jadis was obviously jarred by my conversational shift. "Is that a theoretical question?"

"No. There's a monster living in the wishing well by the newspaper building."

"And you just left it there?"

"Until dark. I can't go after it when someone might see me. He's not doing anything but stinking up the joint and threatening to invite me over for finger foods – which are made of literal fingers, mind you – so I figured I could wait for the cover of darkness to go after him. I just want to know if you know what he is so I don't waste time when it comes to forcing him back to the other side."

"I can't say that I've ever heard of such a creature." Jadis was thoughtful. "It talks?"

"Entire conversations. It used the word 'posh' like it was a normal thing."

"And it just appeared in the well out of nowhere?" Jadis didn't sound thrilled at the possibility.

"It did. I didn't even know it was there until the scent hit me and I went to take a look. He didn't seem surprised to see me. He also didn't appear worried when I told him he couldn't stay and I would be back."

"That's a little ... disconcerting."

That's so not the word I would've used. "It's worrisome, but until I actually try to move him ... and fail ... there isn't much I can do about it."

"Try to get one of the others to help you move him," Jadis instructed. "That way you'll outnumber him should he try something."

"I don't believe my fellow witches are in the mood to help me right now."

"They'll have to get over that." Jadis was the pragmatic sort, so talk of a juvenile argument wasn't about to derail her practical side. "You need to make sure that thing doesn't get comfortable."

"Or start eating babies," I added.

"Definitely. I'll do some research on my end and send it your way if I come up with something. Other than that, the only thing I can offer is my hope that you're victorious."

"I'm sure it will be fine."

"I'm sure it will be, too."

"So, if that's all ... ."

"Just one more thing. When do you think you'll go on your first date with August Taylor? Everyone has a pool going, and I think I should benefit from inside information. I have to put up with you on a weekly basis, so it only seems fair."

I made a face. "Goodnight, Jadis."

"And goodnight to you. Don't worry about the tip. I already know when it's going to happen. Thanks."

And just like that she disconnected and left me with my dark thoughts. What the heck was going on with everyone assuming Augie and I were going to hook up? That was just laughable. I mean ... seriously laughable.

Ugh. My stomach hurts. I hate all this upheaval. It makes me tense.

Fifteen

I had time to burn.

I could have written an article for the newspaper. That would've been the responsible thing to do. Instead I paced my living room, pouted about one of my witchy so-called friends tattling, and constantly found my mind traveling back to Blair Whitney.

Jadis wanted me to focus on my job, which technically consisted of battling back monsters that managed to find a way around the makeshift door we'd erected after the incident. I was supposed to ignore the other types of monsters I regularly ran across. That was on top of my day job as a mild-mannered reporter on the most boring island imaginable. If I could write about the things I really did, that might be entertaining.

It wasn't an option, though.

Kenna, Zola, and Evian believed I was sticking my nose where it didn't belong. They thought I was interested because I discovered the body. That was only part of it. In truth, I sensed that I was supposed to follow the trail of evidence and solve the case. There was something inside of me that demanded I not let go. Some would call it intuition. I wasn't sure I could give it a name. I only knew I couldn't stop now.

"I'm heading to the resort."

Swoops didn't bother raising his head as he snored in his hammock. Tut barely opened one eye before squeezing it shut.

"Don't everyone hop up and down while applauding my work ethic," I grumbled.

"Bring back dinner," Tut called out as I strolled toward the door. "I'm feeling like tuna casserole tonight."

I had never made tuna anything — I hate fish, but love seafood, go figure — and I certainly wasn't going to start now. "That's not going to happen."

Corned beef hash.

"That's not going to happen either unless I can find the low-sodium stuff that will reduce your blood pressure."

Swoops made a derisive sound, and even though his eyes remained closed I was fairly certain he was offering me the bat version of a one-fingered salute. He had only one finger at the tip of his wings, so that was a fair assumption.

"I'll be back when I can." I twisted the door handle. "Keep your eyes and ears open regarding the thing in the wishing well. If you hear it's running around, get word to me at the resort. I'm going to have to handle him before the end of the night, too."

"You can count on us." Tut sounded smug. "Don't forget dinner."

"I said I was going to do it, so I will. Get off my back. You're worse than Jadis."

Corned beef hash!

"Don't make me remove all meat and potato products from this house, Swoops!"

THE RESORT WAS QUIET when I arrived. I managed to sweet talk Dylan into telling me where Blair Whitney's daughter was for the afternoon, and when I found out she was at the mud pits I wanted to curse a brown streak – like the mud I was potentially going to be forced to brave. But then I put on my big-girl panties (I had to because I was forced to settle for granny panties this morning) and made my way to the pits.

I smelled them before I saw them. There were two, although one was a decent distance from the resort, and the first was almost always the one chosen by guests. That's where I found Sheridan Whitney and Rebecca Preston as I cut across the grounds and rounded the corner to the main outdoor area.

I pulled up short, thankful neither woman was looking in my direction, and watched them for a while. They seemed lost in thought, chatty with one another, and entirely oblivious to how they should be acting.

It was an interesting sight.

My original plan was to climb into the mud (which I never wanted to do despite everyone else making yummy girl noises over the healing properties it offered) and weave a little spell to loosen their tongues. It wasn't exactly a truth spell, but it would hopefully be enough to get them talking. Now that I knew exactly where they were, though – and what they were likely to be doing for at least the next hour – I had another idea.

I turned quickly, every intention of returning to the inn so I could infiltrate housekeeping and go through Rebecca's room fueling me, but I pulled up short when Augie stepped into my path. Was he somehow LoJacked to me this week? How did he keep finding me? And why did he keep showing up?

"Augie." I kept my voice low so as not to disturb the

women in the pit. "Are you here spying on the guests? Do you have a mud fetish I don't know about?"

Augie's expression was haughty. "I don't think any of my fetishes have to do with mud. Rum runners, on the other hand ... ." He smirked at my discomfort before turning serious. "What are you doing out here, Skye?"

Eternal Springs wasn't large, but it also wasn't so small that I should've had occasion to run into Augie three times in one day. That was stretching the limitations of feasibility. "I was looking for the source of that smell." That seemed plausible. In fact, it made a lot of sense now that I gave it some thought. "It's definitely coming from here."

Augie's forehead wrinkled as he lifted his chin and scented the air. "I don't smell anything."

"That's because you're used to the stink. Your nose has become accustomed to it."

"I didn't have a problem smelling it at your office."

"And yet I didn't smell it there. It's coming from here."

"See, I think you're full of crap and you're covering for something else," Augie countered. "Because that's the least of my worries — I don't care how many people are walking around town talking about how much you smell — I think you should handle that problem on your own."

Now it was my turn to make a face. "I don't smell."

"Not usually, but your building smelled today. I would call island services to have that checked out if I were you. It could be a sewer break right under your building. That could turn messy."

"I have it under control."

"Great."

"Good."

We lapsed into uncomfortable silence and eyed one another for several minutes. I considered walking away without uttering another word — I simply had no idea what else I was going to say — but Augie had other ideas.

"Are you going to try to question them?"

I glanced over my shoulder to where Sheridan and Rebecca remained lost in conversation. "I was considering it."

"What changed your mind? I mean, you were walking away when I found you."

"Do you want the truth or should I lie?"

Augie was taken aback by the question. "I don't know. Will I be upset with the truth?"

"Probably."

"Can you come up with a convincing lie?"

"Probably."

"Well ... I guess tell me the truth," Augie said after a beat. "I'd rather hear that than a lie, no matter how good you are at spinning a tale."

The truth, huh? He would probably regret that. "I was going to head back to the resort, pretend I was a maid, and go through Rebecca Preston's room."

Augie's mouth dropped open. "I can't believe you just admitted that."

I couldn't either. "I figured she'd be more likely to hide things there than admit the truth to an absolute stranger. I thought it was worth a shot."

Augie made a clucking sound with his tongue as he shook his head. "I don't know whether to be horrified or impressed."

"Impressed."

"It was ballsy for you to admit that."

"But?"

"But I can't let you break into a guest's room to go through her stuff," Augie argued. "It's not right. I mean ... not right at all. I could get fired for that."

"You could."

"Of course I might have already done it myself, in which case it would simply be a wasted effort for you," he added, his grin turning sly.

My interest was officially piqued. "Come again. Are you saying that you broke into a guest's room and went through her stuff? Augie!" I slapped my hand against his arm so hard it jarred him. "You're so much cooler than I thought you were. What did you find?"

Augie's face flushed with color, although I couldn't be certain if it was because he was pleased with my comment or mortified we were suddenly on the same level. "Do you have to be so loud?" He peered around my shoulder to make sure Rebecca and Sheridan didn't hear us. "You'll get me arrested if you're not careful."

I snorted. "How do you figure?"

"What I did is against the law."

"I won't tell if you don't. Er, wait. I won't tell you broke the law if you share the information you found. I'm honestly dying to know."

Augie took a long time making up his mind, running his tongue over his teeth as he internally debated. Finally he exhaled heavily and held up his hands. "I don't even know why I'm fighting this. I want to tell you what I found because I have no one else to talk it over with."

Oh, this had to be good. "And?"

Augie grabbed me by the elbow and tugged to relocate our gossip session, making sure we were completely out of eyesight (and hopefully earshot) should Sheridan and Rebecca look in our direction. He was obviously serious about keeping this quiet.

"I found financial documents in Rebecca Preston's room." He kept his voice low. "They were interesting and confusing at the same time. I'm not an accountant, so it took me longer than it should have to understand what I was looking at. I probably should've paid more attention in high school math."

"Don't beat yourself up, Augie. I'm still waiting to figure out how fractions are going to help me as an adult. People swore up and down I would need to know how to add and subtract them, but I've yet to run into a scenario where that's true."

Augie let loose a "well, duh" face that had me biting back a laugh. "You always manage to turn every conversation to yourself."

"You say that like it's a bad thing."

"It's annoying."

"I'll file that away for the next time you and I want to have a deep and meaningful conversation about me," I shot back. "Tell me what you found in Rebecca's room. I'm practically dying here."

"You have so little patience," Augie muttered as he ran a hand through his dark hair. "That's one of your biggest faults."

"I'm sure you have a whole list of faults where I'm concerned." I poked his stomach to prod him. "Spill."

"Okay, okay." Augie waved my hand away. "I found financial documents. They belong to Charles Whitney. I'm not sure where Rebecca got them, but she has them and they contain notations, as if she had a lawyer go through them to explain things."

Hmm. "Were the notations written in crayon or something? I mean, I haven't spent a lot of time with her, but she doesn't seem all that bright."

"Not crayon, but they were broken down to a very basic level. As if she specifically asked for it to be done that way."

"Okay, I guess that makes sense. What did you find in there?"

"Charles Whitney is nowhere near as rich as everyone

seems to believe he is." Augie rubbed his hands together as he warmed to the story. It was as if having permission to be bad elevated his mood. "He's wealthy, don't get me wrong, but the stories we hear on the news don't tell the whole tale."

"Can you expand on that?"

"Sure. It seems that Charles lost a lot of money in the stock market in 2008. We're talking millions. His worth before the crash was around the fifteen-million mark. Now he's only worth two million."

I tilted my head to the side, considering. "Two million is still a lot to most people."

"It is, but from what I read that money is mostly tied up in his business. It's not liquid. He doesn't have access to it. He's had to sell two boats, his share in a private plane and a New York City apartment to keep his other personal assets afloat."

"She had all of that in her room?" I had trouble wrapping my brain around it. "I can't imagine Charles Whitney providing her with those documents."

"I can't either."

"That means she either stole them when he wasn't looking or got her hands on them through alternative means," I mused, tapping my bottom lip as I ran through the possible scenarios. "Maybe the daughter got them for her."

"Or maybe the daughter had access to them because her father shared his financial difficulties with her and Rebecca stole them from Sheridan. That's also a possibility."

So many possibilities. I preferred having one clear-cut answer. As it stood, I thought both Charles and Rebecca were likely suspects in Blair's death. Given how Charles acted when he thought I was Rebecca, I didn't believe that was truly the case.

"Would killing Blair have helped Charles' financial problems?" I asked.

Augie's lips curved. "I was wondering if you would ask that. It turns out Rebecca had access to one other document. It was a copy of a life insurance policy for Blair Whitney for five million dollars ... and it was to be split between Charles and Sheridan."

Huh. I wasn't surprised. "So there was a good motive for Charles to off his wife."

"There was," Augie confirmed. "There was also good reason for Rebecca to do it if she thought Charles would officially propose once the dust settled. There was a notation on the documents — which makes me think Rebecca asked a series of explicit questions that she wanted answers to — and whoever wrote in the margins warned her not to sign a prenuptial agreement if she wanted to get any money out of a future marriage."

Ding, ding, ding! We had a winner. "So Rebecca thought that Charles would be flush with funds again after Blair's death. If they waited a few months to get married, that would keep people from being suspicious."

"Basically."

My excitement of moments before crashed. "Of course Charles could have all the money — except for Sheridan's share — and not have to share it with anyone if he doesn't marry again."

"That is also true."

Well, crap. I was right back where I started. "I don't know which idea makes the most sense to me. I haven't spent enough time with Rebecca to ascertain if she's smart enough to pull something like this off."

"Originally I would've said no, but I'm not so certain now," Augie said. "I think she's smarter than anyone gives her credit for."

"And what about the daughter? Do you think she knows her best friend is sleeping with her father?"

"I can't answer that. Sheridan has been quiet since her mother's death."

"And yet they're still here," I pointed out. "I don't know about you, but if my mother died at a resort I'd be on my way home as quickly as possible. I wouldn't hang around taking mud baths with a potential suspect, that's for sure."

"Unless Sheridan doesn't know what her father has been up to," Augie pointed out. "I haven't been able to get close enough to talk to her more than twice since it happened – the assistant is militant about protecting her – but she doesn't seem as if she's all that tied into what's happening with her father. She seems oblivious, or maybe I'm just intuiting that because I feel sorry for her. She seems to be the only one in this little group that isn't completely obnoxious and hateful."

I could see that. "I don't know what to make about it. Maybe I should head over and talk to them."

"Under normal circumstances I'd think that's a bad idea, but we're running out of time. Abigail is getting pressure from the state to declare the death murder or accidental. No matter what Buddy wants, I don't think she's going to say it's an accident. Once she calls it murder, I can officially start questioning people."

"And once you do that the guilty party is likely to run right out of your jurisdiction," I finished.

"That's it exactly."

"Well ... crap!" I pressed my lips together and turned my attention to the setting sun. "I think that's about the worst thing that could happen to us."

Even as I said it, I knew it was a mistake. I'd totally jinxed the operation. Now things were going to get worse. I could feel it.

And, as if on cue, Swoops glided in out of nowhere and started hooting.

"Isn't that your bat?" Augie narrowed his eyes. "What's he doing out here?"

That was a very good question. "I don't know. Sometimes he likes following me around. That's probably what he's doing now."

I believed that for a full two seconds, right until Swoops' brain started broadcasting on all frequencies.

The monster is out and coming this way. He's close. He's going to eat us all. Run for your lives!

Yep. I totally jinxed us.

Sixteen

The monster was coming. Tim was out of the well and moving. And apparently he was heading in this direction. But ... why? And, more importantly, how was I going to get Augie out of here before he saw the smelly menace?

"What's wrong with you?" Augie detected the change in my demeanor, but because he couldn't hear Swoops he had no idea about my inner turmoil. "Are you sick?"

Sick in the head. Sick to death of monsters. Sick to my stomach because the idea of Augie getting hurt made me physically ill. How did that even happen?

"I'm fine," I lied, swallowing hard as I slowly swiveled to scan the woods to the west. If Tim was coming, it would most likely be from that direction. "The smell from the mud pits is just getting to me."

"I've told you ten times that smell is not from the mud pits. I ... ." Augie trailed off and wrinkled his nose. "What is that?"

I didn't need to ask what he was talking about. I could smell it, too. "It's the mud pit. I told you that."

"But ... it didn't smell like this a few minutes ago."

"It did. You just missed it."

"How could I miss that? Good grief." Augie pinched his nose and bent over at the waist. "I think I might pass out. That is some rank stuff."

"Suck it up." I smacked him on the back hard enough to cause an echo, my mind working overtime as I tried to figure a way to clear the area without alerting Augie to what was about to happen. "You know what? If you're feeling lightheaded, how do you think they're feeling?" I gestured toward Rebecca and Sheridan. "You should get them out of here."

"I'm sure they're not going to want to stay." Augie gagged while staring at the ground. "I seriously think I might throw up. I don't care if you find it unmanly. I have a weak stomach."

He wasn't the only one. That was the problem. Er, well, at least one problem. "It's not unmanly."

"Then what's your problem?"

"I'm a sympathetic puker."

Augie barked out a laugh that ended in a sound that caused my stomach to churn for a different reason. "Oh, that's just ... priceless."

"Don't make that noise."

"What noise?" He made it again and I actually felt myself go green.

"That noise! Knock it off!"

Augie made the noise again, but this time I could tell he was faking it so I didn't have the same visceral reaction. I elbowed his stomach, causing him to cough hard enough that he legitimately gagged, which caused the feelings of revulsion to return.

"Knock it off!" I was deathly serious as I straightened. "I didn't tell you my deepest and darkest secret so you could taunt me with it."

Augie was dubious. "That's your deepest and darkest secret?"

In an odd way, it was. It was certainly the one that made me feel weakest. "Yes. Do you have a problem with that?"

"No. I'm just surprised you told me."

He wasn't the only one. "Yes, well ... ." I was wasting time. I needed to get Augie out of here. If I didn't, he could end up hurt. He could also find out my other secret if I wasn't careful, and that would end poorly for more than just me. "You should get them out of here, Augie. They could get faint or lightheaded because of the smell."

"Also, if the mud really does smell that bad maybe something toxic is leaking into it," Augie noted. "We don't want guests getting sick right on the heels of a suspicious death. I'll nudge them to the spa, tell them there was a garbage spill in town and the wind is blowing this way."

The wind. Hmm. "That's a really good idea. I'll help you."

CONVINCING SHERIDAN AND Rebecca to leave the mud pit was easy. The smell was nauseating and they were eager to partake in the free drinks Augie offered. Because they could do it in an air-conditioned environment that didn't smell like a professional football team's jockstrap pile only added to the enticement.

Augie didn't look over his shoulder as he herded them to the resort. I couldn't be sure if he forgot I was there or merely let his work ethic take charge. It hardly mattered, but part of me was bothered that he seemed to forget my presence.

The other part was profoundly glad because my enemy detached from the trees mere minutes after they vacated the area.

"What happened to your boyfriend?"

Now that he was walking on two legs Tim was a sight to behold. He was almost seven feet tall, with squat legs that reminded me of a crocodile and a scaly torso rippling with muscles. He looked strong. Most hell beasts do. I wasn't particularly frightened of that strength, but I wasn't keen to get into a physical battle. This fight would have to be conducted on the magical playing field.

"I don't have a boyfriend." I maintained an even distance from Tim as he circled. His short legs gave the impression he wouldn't be fast, but he seemed so sure of himself that I figured that wasn't the case. "If you're talking about the guy who was just here, he's head of resort security and was simply doing his job."

"He was doing more than that." Tim looked smug. "He was watching you."

"He was *talking* to me. We have common interests right now."

"That may very well be true, but he was here for you. Do you know how I know that?" He didn't wait for me to answer, instead barreling forward. "I know because his heartbeat changed rhythm when you said something funny ... or when you hit his back. It wasn't that you hurt him. It was that you touched him and he found it exciting."

That was the most ludicrous thing I'd ever heard. "We were trying not to vomit. That's not really the stuff of great romance."

"If you say so." Tim started moving again, short steps, his eyes never leaving my face. "Why did you get the others out? You could have used them as fodder, but you seemed intent on removing them from the situation. I don't understand why."

"I can't let you eat them."

"Why not?"

"That's not how things work on this side. I know you're

used to a different world, but I can't let you ruin this one in a quest to make a new home. It's simply ... not allowed. This world has rules."

"Every world has rules," Tim pointed out. "I like this world because the rules are ... softer."

"Just like the babies, huh?"

"I was joking about that. Babies aren't the only thing on the menu. I find adults just as tasty."

"Good to know." I chewed my bottom lip as Tim swished his tail. The sudden movement caused my muscles to tense, but I didn't adopt a fighting stance. I didn't want to give Tim reason to pounce. "You can't stay here. You know that, right?"

"I won't leave. This is my new home."

"You won't have a choice in the matter." I moved again when Tim tried to inch closer at an angle. "I can't let you stay. That's the biggest rule in my world, the one I can't break."

"And you think you're strong enough to take me, do you?"

"I think you've underestimated me," I replied. "You recognize I'm a threat. That's why you found me. Don't bother denying it. You didn't come out here for the mud pit girls. You were looking for me. That's why you went by my house first."

"Did the flying rat tell you that?"

No rat! No rat!

Swoops glided above our heads, staying close in case I needed his help anchoring my magic but making sure not to get close enough to Tim that he might accidentally turn into a delicious appetizer.

"It talks," Tim growled, lifting his eyes to the sky. "How did I miss that? Do all rats here talk?"

No rat! Swoops was furious.

"Don't let him bother you, Swoops," I ordered. "Everyone who is important knows you're not a rat."

"He's a flying rat," Tim corrected. "You didn't answer my

question about him. Do all rats here talk? If so I'll have to find an exterminator."

I realized what he was doing a split second before he moved. He was trying to knock me off my guard, delay my reflexes. It didn't work, of course. He was hardly the first monster that had crossed my path.

I was ready when Tim extended his claws and pounced. I hopped up, allowing my air magic to build and give me some lift. I flew over his head, flipping as I turned mid-air and landing with a solid bounce in my calves. I didn't need to see the surprise in Tim's eyes when he realized I was gone. I also didn't need to wait for him to get his bearings and try again.

It was my turn to attack.

I extended my hands and planted them on his back, my lips already moving as I conjured a tiny tsunami to encircle him.

"Two worlds, one door. One creature, no more." It wasn't my best rhyming work, but I didn't have much time to think. It worked. I could tell the second I took a step back and the whipping winds started wailing.

Tim twisted and contorted, his eyes flashing fire as they widened. "No!"

"I told you. You can't be here. You should've listened to me. There are less painful ways to force a trip to the other side. This was your choice, not mine."

"You witch!" Tim screamed as the wind whirled so fast it distorted his features. "I will be back."

"I'm looking forward to it, Tim. Try to take a bath before the next trip. That scent is a dead giveaway."

I barely got the words out before Tim disappeared, the wind remaining for a moment before dissipating, licking my hair and blowing it away from my face before the sun returned and illuminated the clearing.

Well, that was one less thing on my to-do list.

I WAS EXHAUSTED ON my way home so I decided to stop at the beachside tiki bar for a drink to calm my nerves. Anchors Away was a kitschy bar that offered sand, a cool breeze, twinkle lights, and a bevy of locals looking to hook up. I was open for all of it tonight ... except for the hooking up, of course.

Captain Mack Shakes (so not his real name) manned the bar. He was all bluster and drunken Johnny Depp impressions when tourists were around. When it was just locals, he was a normal guy. Thankfully he didn't feel the need to put on a show tonight.

"Hey, Skye." Mack beamed as I snagged a stool. "I haven't seen you around these parts in almost two weeks. What's the special occasion?"

"I just want a stiff drink – and no singing."

Mack snorted. "I heard about your singing last night. I also heard you weren't alone."

Great. I should've known that was coming. "I had a little too much to drink last night. I'm not going to let it happen again. You have my word."

"You're close enough to walk home. I don't care if you get drunk. Just don't sing. I heard that you're so bad when it comes to hitting the right notes the deaf want to ban you from karaoke."

"Oh, you're so funny," I drawled, rolling my eyes until they landed on the daiquiri machine. "Give me something fruity."

"You've got it." Mack left me to my deep thoughts. I only jolted from them when he slid a piña colada in front of me at the same moment I felt a presence move in at my right.

I already had the straw in my mouth when I turned and found Augie watching me with curious eyes. "Are you following me?"

"No. I always come here on Saturdays. Everyone knows that. I think you're following me."

"Only you would think that." I sipped my drink and watched as he ordered something blue from Mack. I was curious about how the rest of his day went, but leery of asking. Thankfully Augie took the decision out of my hands.

"Where did you go?"

"When?"

"You know when." Augie thanked Mack for his drink and twirled the small umbrella in the glass for a beat. "I thought you were with us right up until we hit the resort, and then I realized you were gone. Why did you stay behind?"

"I just wanted to see if I could find the source of the smell. I couldn't. It seemed to dissipate, though. It was really weird."

"It *was* weird," Augie agreed. "I went back out there looking for you and the smell was completely gone, except for a strange remnant that I could only smell in the field to the west of the pit. It wasn't strong."

"That's good, right?"

"It is."

"Well, then you have nothing to complain about." For lack of anything better to do, I sucked on my straw until I started getting a strong case of brain freeze, and then rubbed my forehead and tried to pretend I didn't hear Augie chuckling. "It's not funny."

"It's a little funny." Augie took a dainty sip of his drink, as if showing me the proper way to do it, and then turned serious. "I was a little worried about you, Skye. I know that scent could be naturally occurring – I'm not sure how, but it's possible – but it was powerful enough to knock someone out. I thought maybe that's what happened to you."

That was kind of sweet ... and annoying. "I'm more than capable of taking care of myself."

"I didn't say you weren't."

"And yet you checked on me anyway," I pointed out. "Did you really think I stayed behind to inhale noxious fumes because I'd somehow find that fun?"

"No, but you didn't go home and you weren't at the newspaper office. I had every reason to be worried."

I furrowed my brow. "You checked my house?"

"I did. The only thing I found was that freaking bat you insist on calling a pet. He was flying around the living room making this weird chirping. I almost thought he was yelling at your cat. By the way, when did you get a cat?"

"I don't have a cat."

"That hairless stray that bites people when they try to pet it ... or wrap it in a sweater ... was in your living room. It was sleeping in your laundry."

Ugh. I hate that freaking cat! "He gets in the house somehow and makes himself at home. He's not my pet. He's a tiny hairless terrorist who takes over my space when he feels like it."

Augie's lips curved. "Ah. Well, the cats on this island are all kinds of weird. I guess that shouldn't surprise me."

"No, they're psychos. My only pet is Swoops. I promise you that."

"Good to know." Augie kicked back in his chair and smiled. "By the way, when I stopped at the newspaper office I thought I smelled something in your wishing well."

Uh-oh. "Did you look inside? Maybe an animal crawled in there and died."

"It looked empty, although the water was kind of green."

"Huh." Seriously, what did he expect me to say to that? "I can't really say I've ever paid much attention to the well."

"I have. I used to make wishes all the time when I was a kid."

"Oh, yeah? What did you wish for?"

"When I was little I wished for a Nintendo. When I was older I wished for a pretty girl to play Nintendo with."

Now it was my turn to laugh. "Well, at least you were consistent. What would you wish for today?"

"I don't know, but something tells me whatever it is wouldn't be nearly as easy to handle as those earlier wishes." As if to prove there was double meaning to his words, he slid his cocktail umbrella behind my ear. "Not nearly as easy to handle at all."

Oh, geez! Why must things always get complicated at the exact moment I think they're going to get easier?

"Give me another drink," I called out, resigned.

"When will the singing start?" Mack asked, winking. "I heard you guys are great at duets."

"I heard that, too." Augie didn't seem nearly as upset by the statement as I felt. "We'll definitely have to polish up our act."

Now that was a frightening thought.

Seventeen

I didn't mean to stay for more than one drink. My original plan was to drink my piña colada and then head home for a good night's sleep. I needed to think through my strategy for approaching Sheridan Whitney now that my original idea turned out to be a bust.

That's not how things went.

"Do you want to take a walk on the beach?" Augie used a cocktail napkin to wipe the corners of his mouth before standing and reaching for his wallet.

The question seemed to come from nowhere so I had no idea how to answer. One moment we'd been having a perfectly snarky time at the bar – Mack making a fuss over our singing and dancing skills, which he'd apparently seen video footage of – and the banter was more playful than flirty. Now, when I least expected it, he was asking me to walk on the beach. That seemed more flirty than playful.

"I don't know," I said after a beat. "I should probably get home. I have some thinking to do if I expect to find a way to get close to Sheridan Whitney and ask her about her best friend, a woman who very well might've had a hand in killing her mother."

"Okay." Augie blinked twice and shook his head. "Or we could take a walk and talk about how best to approach her together. You know ... I mean ... two heads are clearly better than one."

It was a lame attempt. I'd had three drinks over the course of two hours, which meant a lame attempt wouldn't work on me. There was absolutely no way I could allow whatever this was to continue.

"Okay." The single word was out of my mouth before I even grasped what I was about to say. I hopped down from my chair and reached for my purse. "Just let me settle up with Mack."

"I've got it," Augie said hurriedly.

"Oh, no, I can't let you do that."

Augie gently placed his hand on mine to stop me from unzipping my purse. "I've got it. It's three drinks. It's not as if that's going to break me."

I thought about arguing further, but knew it would simply serve as a way to draw attention to us. "I guess that's okay. Um ... thank you."

"No problem."

I waited for Augie to square up with Mack, doing my best to ignore the gregarious bartender when he shot me an enthusiastic thumbs-up before heading down the beach. It was harder to pretend I didn't know what was going through his head when he called after us.

"Be safe," Mack yelled to our backs. "Have fun. Wear protection, Augie! I can't imagine how obnoxious a kid with half your genes and half Skye's genes would be."

It was a good thing it was dark because my cheeks burned so hot I knew there was no way Augie could miss it if we had proper lighting. Thankfully he seemed as nervous as me as he chuckled and shook his head.

"That Mack is a trip, huh?"

That's not the word I'd use for him. "He's ... something," I said, taking a moment to lift my head and inhale the salty air. "I love this time of year. I love walking on the beach and dipping my toes in the shallows. Not too far or anything, but I love squinching my toes in the sand as the night tide rolls in."

"So, let's do that." Augie plopped down on the sand and reached for his shoes. "I like a nice walk on the beach, too."

I stared at his profile, my stomach twisting as my head started lobbing vulgarities at me due to my rather unnatural thoughts. "You're kind of cute when you want to be."

Augie snapped his head in my direction, the smile that flitted across his face a mixture of pleasant surprise and mirth. "You're kind of cute, too."

I wrinkled my nose as I lowered myself to the ground and tugged off my sandals. "You didn't always think I was cute," I pointed out. "You used to tell me I was ugly even for a nun when I first started going to Eternal Springs High School."

Augie balked. "I never called you ugly."

"You did. You said you could see why I wanted to be a nun because with a face like mine I could never get a husband."

Augie's shoulders sagged as mortification slid across his face. "I am so sorry."

I wasn't used to this contrite creature sitting next to me. I didn't know what to make of him. I much preferred the cocky Augie I more regularly saw during my daily travels. "It's not the end of the world. I clearly survived."

"Still ... that's not how I felt. Not even then."

"Oh, yeah? How did you feel?" It seemed an odd conversation to have given our location and yet the progression felt somehow natural. Augie and I had spent so much time hating one another that the shift to liking one another – er, well, at least working together – opened up a mountain of questions about the past.

"We were all surprised when we heard you were coming to school with us. Everyone used to be fascinated with St. Joan of Arc – mostly because you guys weren't allowed to hang out in town without a chaperone – but no one ever got to spend time with you, so the only thing we knew is what our imaginations led us to believe."

I guess that made sense. I never thought about it from Augie's point of view. "What were you told when we started attending school with you?"

"Well, for starters, the school burning down was big news." Augie let some sand filter between his fingers. "The night it happened, I remember my mother waking me up and insisting that we had to run out there. There was a real fear that girls would die in the fire."

Hmm. "I remember that night differently. You were outside looking in. I was inside desperately trying to get out."

Augie slid me a sidelong look. "What do you mean?"

I couldn't tell him everything. He couldn't handle everything. "I was in the basement when the first alarm sounded. I was awake, but the alarm jolted me all the same."

"Were you alone?"

"No. Kenna, Evian, and Zola were with me."

"Why doesn't that surprise me?"

I shrugged. "The basement filled with smoke quickly." Mostly because one of the monsters that made it through the gate breathed fire and headed for the curtains first. "I knew the space really well, but I couldn't see through the smoke."

Augie leaned closer. "You don't have to talk about this if you don't want to."

I waved off his concern. "It's fine. It was a long time ago."

"And yet you look like you're re-living it."

"I re-live it all the time." Sure, it's mostly in dreams, but I've re-lived it other times as well. "We had to call out to each other. Three of us found each other quickly, but it took longer to find Evian. We did, though, and then we had to find the stairs."

To my surprise, Augie reached over and carefully gathered my hand in his. "From outside, we could hear the building going. We heard screams inside, and people wanted to run and help, but we were ordered back because it wasn't safe.

"I still remember when the first group of girls came through," he continued. "They were crying, but all together in a line. I thought that was everybody even though I knew it wasn't. I'd seen you and the older girls before and knew you weren't outside with the first group, yet I assumed you were safe somehow.

"That only lasted until a woman started shrieking at the fire chief, who also happened to be the barber at the time," he said. "She had short hair. It was brown and stood up. I don't know why I remember that. She was yelling that four girls were still missing. That's when I realized you were one of them."

I was taken aback. "You knew who I was before the fire?"

He nodded. "I saw you around. I was a teenager. We used to hang out in the woods to drink a little beer now and then. We found a spot where we could watch you guys in the courtyard and we used to hang out and lament the fact that you were going to become nuns. We thought it was a waste."

I didn't want to laugh. It was a serious moment, after all. I couldn't stop myself. "That's kind of funny."

"Your hair stood out. It was so light and it seemed to have a mind of its own when you walked. You know how people say models walk as if they have wind in their hair? You always walked that way."

I was absurdly touched by the admission. "I didn't know

you were there the night of the fire. I don't remember much about it other than we were frightened until we found our way out."

"They were making plans to search for you." Augie adopted a far-off expression. "I told my mom I wanted to help search for you, but she told me to stop acting crazy. I was determined to try. Then we heard this noise — as if the building was going to fall in on itself — and the fire chief started yelling for everyone to get back.

"The woman who said you were still inside yelled ... something," he continued. "I swear it was a language I didn't recognize. Then, as if by magic, the four of you stumbled through the front door at the same time part of the roof toward the back of the building collapsed. You just made it out."

I remembered things a little differently. The woman was Jadis, and she yelled to cast a spell to clear the smoke so we wouldn't become overwhelmed and not be able to find our way out. "It was a tense evening," I conceded. "It's one of those times I'll never be able to forget."

"Yeah, well, when word came down that some of you were going to start going to school with us it was big news," Augie explained. "You have to understand, all that we knew about you is that you were going to be nuns. When you showed up at school and seemed relatively normal — I mean kind of normal, not totally normal — no one knew what to make of it.

"We thought you would wear those outfits, habits, and stuff, and we were afraid to hang out with you," he continued. "Everyone thought you were pretty and wanted to ask you out, but my mother said you guys were already married to God so I shouldn't push it because I couldn't compete."

He was so earnest I could do nothing but press my lips together to keep from laughing.

"I can tell what you're thinking," Augie grumbled. "You

think I'm being an idiot." He kept his hand on top of mine, either because he forgot to move it or because he liked the feel of skin against skin. "I kept waiting for you to magically turn into a nun after graduation. I thought you'd leave. Then I thought they would rebuild the school. But you stayed and didn't magically turn into a nun."

"You sound disappointed about that."

"I don't think 'disappointed' is the right word. I was more confused."

"You didn't act confused," I pointed out. "You always poked me whenever you saw me, kind of like you were feeding off my animosity."

"I was." Augie turned sheepish. "You know how they say some people don't care how they get attention – whether it's good or bad – as long as they get some sort of reaction? That's how I always felt about you."

Was he baring his soul here? I wasn't sure I could take that. "Augie ... ."

"I really wish you would call me August, at least when I'm working. No one takes a guy named 'Augie' seriously."

"First, your name is Augie." I had no intention of backing down on that. "The name fits you. August sounds stuffy; you're not stuffy. You're fun and annoying and you know how to irritate people. That sounds like an Augie to me."

He made an annoyed face. "I think you're the only one who believes that."

"Oh, puh-leez." I rolled my eyes. "I'm hardly the only one on the island calling you that. It's part of who you are. It's too late to change it. There's nothing wrong with being an Augie. It makes you more ... approachable."

"You don't ever want to approach me."

Was that what was bothering him? "That's because you always tease me and pick a fight."

"You're the one who picks fights."

"No, it's you."

"Don't ruin this." Augie's tone was almost a growl. "I'm willing to take some responsibility for the fact that we always bicker, but you have to take some of it, too. It's not all me. You're ready to argue before I even open my mouth sometimes."

He had a point. "That's because you're good at fighting."

Augie was taken aback. "That almost sounded like a compliment."

"It was." We were at a point of no return. I could feel the energy crackling between us. I could turn back and erect a wall big enough that neither of us would be able to climb over it or crawl under it, or I could push forward. The question was, what did I really want?

The answer was simple. There was no going back. It was already too late, although I had no idea how that had happened. "I'm the sort of person who likes to debate, Augie. It's part of my personality. I can't shake it and I'm pretty sure I don't want to."

Augie appeared bemused. "Are you saying you don't want to be a nicer individual?"

"You wouldn't like me if I was nicer. Nicer is boring."

"Not always." Augie lifted our hands and I realized somehow we'd linked fingers when I wasn't aware. "Sometimes you're kind of sweet without realizing it."

I knit my eyebrows. "Augie, I'm not sure this is a good idea."

He didn't seem surprised by the statement. "I'm not sure it is either. I think there's a reason I've always been fascinated by you, though. I think sometimes that fascination made me mean when it wasn't exactly fair to you, but ... I can't seem to shake this feeling."

"What feeling is that?"

"That if I don't go after you you'll never come after me."

It was a simple statement, but it was loaded with emotions I wasn't sure I could handle. "And what if it blows up in our faces?"

"Then we'll go back to being mean to each other. It's not a big risk when you really think about it."

It felt big. It felt so big my heart actually sighed. "I need to think about it."

"Okay." Augie took me by surprise when he hopped to his feet, dragging me with him as he moved toward the water. "While you're thinking about it, I thought we might do that sinking thing in the water. You know the thing where you stand and let the surf wash over you to the point your feet are buried in the sand when the water recedes? I want to do that."

The shift in his demeanor threw me for a loop. "That's what you want to do?"

"Yup."

"But ... I might need more than an hour splashing around the ocean to think this through."

"Oh, you're definitely going to need more time than that," Augie agreed. He seemed calm, almost happy, as he stuck his toe in the water. "If you decide this isn't for you there won't be anything I can do about it. You'll walk away and we'll go back to being whatever it is we were before. There won't be beach walks in that world, so I want to do this now."

He was painfully adorable when he wanted to be. How had I never noticed that before? "Okay, but if you try anything funny I'll have to drown you."

Augie snorted. "You wish you could drown me."

Not really and yet ... kind of.

"You're not strong enough to take me anyway." Augie was all bravado and false courage.

"Oh, I could drown you if I wanted," I warned. "I'm stronger than I look."

"I've never doubted that, but ... I think you'll have to prove it to me."

"Fine."

Augie let loose a war whoop before releasing my hand and sloshing into the water. I couldn't figure out what he was doing until a wall of salted liquid smacked me in the face. I licked my lips and pushed my hair from my face as I studied him.

"You'll pay for that," I warned.

"I certainly hope so. That's why I did it."

"Then you'd better start running."

Augie shook his head, that charming grin of his coming out to play. "I favor my chances."

Terrifyingly enough, I was starting to favor them, too.

Eighteen

I was wired when I got home. Augie offered to walk me, but I knew that was a bad idea. We were both soaked, which meant my top was clinging to what few curves I had. His shirt was clinging to him, too, and I had the distinct impression that I would like what I saw if he took that shirt off, and if he walked me home the odds of that shirt disappearing in a typhoon of hands and tongues were high.

I wasn't ready for that. I was being honest when I said I needed to think things through. If Augie and I really did become involved – something I never saw happening until the past forty-eight hours or so – then eventually he would have to find out the truth. I wasn't sure what that would do to him.

For starters, he'd been living under the assumption that I was going to be a nun. The truth could cause everything he believed about me, what I was doing in Eternal Springs in the first place, to come tumbling down. When you added the magic factor, Augie might not be able to take it. He would most likely run before we even got started and then things would return to how they were ... except he would have information to hold over my head or possibly share with the other residents.

It was all a convoluted mess and I couldn't see a way for it to work out for either of us. Despite that, deep down, I wanted to try. There was something about him that called to me. It wasn't a recent thing, either. I think I was always attracted to him, which is why I was especially mean and argumentative whenever he came around.

What? Some people bat their eyelashes and twirl hair when attracted to a guy. I hurl insults. It's who I am.

I stopped at the house long enough to change into dry clothes and braid my hair. Then I decided to take a walk. I needed to clear my head. Augie was clouding things. I still had a murder to solve and I was doubtful I would have much time to do it.

I didn't put up a fight when Swoops slipped out ahead of me and the hairless cat followed at my heels. I didn't even know Tut was in the house when I'd changed. He probably liked watching me or something. Ugh, there's nothing worse than a perverted cat.

Where are we going?

Swoops was a fan of nighttime excursions. I could practically feel his enthusiasm as I strode toward the path at the back of the house. It led into the woods and was ultimately a shortcut to the resort. I didn't know what I expected to find there, but anything was better than sitting at home and stressing over a potential relationship with Augie. I needed to focus on something constructive ... like getting close to Sheridan Whitney. If anyone had the lowdown on her father's relationship with her best friend, it was her.

"The resort. I want to see if I can find the daughter of the murder victim."

"To what end?" Tut asked, his eyes gleaming as he surveyed the foliage. "What do you think she can tell you?"

I shrugged, noncommittal. "I'm not sure. I have trouble believing it's possible for Sheridan not to know what was going on."

"Why would she remain friends with someone who was trying to break up her parents' marriage?"

I should've been surprised at Tut's knowledge of the case, but the hairless little creep was a master at ferreting out information. Obviously he'd been keeping his ears to the ground. "Maybe she didn't like her father and thought her mother would be better off without him."

"Or maybe she didn't like her mother and thought the same," Tut noted. "Still, even if a child recognizes an abusive parent for what he or she is, they don't usually want a friend to enter the picture and potentially become a stepmother."

He had a point. "I haven't been able to get close enough to talk to her. If I could get a feel for her, I might be able to sort this out. It doesn't make sense that Blair Whitney would want her husband's mistress with her on vacation. I mean ... I get being cruel. I get off on being mean sometimes."

"You don't say," Tut drawled.

I ignored his sarcasm. "Bringing a mistress along for the ride has to be uncomfortable for both parties. Rebecca wouldn't be the only one upset about the situation. Even if she was getting off on the power trip, Blair had to hate her life during this spa visit because Rebecca was a constant reminder of what her husband was doing."

"I see where you're coming from and raise you another question," Tut said. "Why would Blair allow Rebecca to bring her mother with her? Lena gave Rebecca a lifeline that Blair shouldn't have wanted if she was simply out to torture Rebecca."

That was another fair point. "I don't know what to make of any of it. If I hated someone I certainly wouldn't want to bring him or her on vacation."

"What about August Taylor?"

My shoulders stiffened at the question. "What does Augie have to do with this conversation?"

"I'm merely curious." Tut swished his tail and stared hard into a clump of bushes. "Rabbit."

"If you kill a rabbit I'll force you to wear its fur to cover your freaky hairless body," I warned. "Leave the rabbit alone."

"Rabbits are blights."

"You're a blight."

"And you're crabby." Tut kept walking, ignoring the rabbit, although I didn't miss the way his ears twitched when he lifted his nose to scent the air. He was a creepy little thing. "Are you crabby because August didn't come home with you?"

Was that a real question? "I'm crabby because a woman died and I want to know who killed her."

"You're crabby because you like August and you think your life would be simpler if you didn't," Tut corrected. "If we're going to have a conversation, at least be honest."

"You want honesty? I hate you."

Tut was imperious. "No, you don't."

"Don't tell me how I feel."

"I think you need someone to tell you how to feel," Tut shot back. "You're too closed off. If you don't let someone else in you'll be a pain in the butt for the rest of your life. August will be good for you. I think you should give it a shot."

"Like I'm going to take advice from a cat," I muttered.

Augie and Skye sitting in a tree. Swoops was a twittering mess. *K-I-S-S-I-N-G.*

"If you ever sing that song again I will bar corned beef hash from the house," I threatened, causing Swoops to instantly go silent.

"She's making that up," Tut said after a beat. "She's mean

on the outside and a marshmallow on the inside. She'll never stop buying you corned beef hash."

I shot him a dark look. "I'm going to take you to the animal shelter and put you up for adoption if you're not careful."

"Go ahead. See where it gets you."

He sounded so sure of himself that I immediately backed off. "I don't understand why you guys even came along on this little excursion. It's not like something exciting is going to happen."

"You never know." Tut was the smug sort and that's how he appeared now. "You might get lucky without even realizing it."

"That would be nice, but I doubt it."

"Have faith," Tut suggested. "A sunnier outlook might do wonders for your reputation."

"I happen to like my reputation."

"No one likes your reputation."

I held up my hand to silence him. "I'm done talking to you for the night. You no longer exist to me."

Tut made a noise that suspiciously sounded as though he was going to cough up a hairball, which was ridiculous because he didn't have any hair. "We'll see where that gets you."

"I hate it when you say things like that."

"That's why I say them."

THE RESORT LOOKED quiet. Swoops immediately peeled off and headed toward the mud pit. That's where the best bugs hang out. At least that's what he told me when I bothered to listen to his long and convoluted stories about hunting down dinner.

Tut drifted toward some bushes on the far side of the

parking lot. I could see him but was happy not to be forced to keep up a conversation I didn't want to be part of. I was debating checking out the resort bar when I noticed a figure walking along the sidewalk. It was a woman, and at first I thought she was talking to herself. After a few moments I realized she was on a cell phone ... and that she was someone I might find interest in interrogating.

"We're leaving tomorrow afternoon. We wanted to be out in the morning, but there are no ferries leaving until after one. I can't wait to get out of here."

Rebecca Preston was dressed down in casual yoga pants and a simple T-shirt. She seemed oblivious to my presence and lost in her own little world.

"No, we still don't know exactly what happened. The security guy wants to talk to us before we leave, but Mom called her attorney and he says we don't have to. The faster we get out of here, the better. I don't understand why we stayed in the first place. But it was Sheridan's decision, and I couldn't really put up a fight given what happened to Blair."

Rebecca listened as the speaker on the other end of the call said something. "It doesn't really matter, does it? I'll be home tomorrow. I need you to pick me up at the airport. The faster I get away from Sheridan and my mother, the better."

Another pause.

"Great. I'll text you as soon as we land. I'm looking forward to seeing you."

Rebecca disconnected her phone and stared at the night sky. She still hadn't seen me, and I couldn't decide if that was good or bad. I finally made up my mind and took a step toward her. If she really was leaving tomorrow I might not have another chance to question her.

"Excuse me."

Rebecca jolted at the sound of my voice, swiveling quickly.

I held up my hands in a placating manner, doing my best to appear innocent and non-confrontational.

"Sorry. I didn't mean to frighten you." I was sure the smile I pasted on my face came off more deranged than trustworthy, but there was nothing I could do about that. "I just wanted to ask you a question."

"You wanted to ask me a question?" Rebecca lifted her eyebrows and glanced over her shoulder, as if expecting someone else to be there. "I don't know what I can tell you," she said finally as she turned back. "I'm not local, so if you're lost there's nothing I can do for you."

"I'm local and I'm not lost."

"Oh." My answer clearly didn't put Rebecca at ease. "What do you want?"

A normal person would've eased into the heavier questions, but I was tired and working on a timetable. If Rebecca was offended by what I was about to ask she would tell me. She didn't seem the type to play games. Er, well, other than sleeping with her best friend's father in order to get her hands on his family's money, that is.

"Does Sheridan know you're having an affair with her father?" I blurted out the question and waited for Rebecca to melt down. Instead, she looked confused and maybe a little panicked.

"What are you asking?"

I decided to give her both barrels. "I'm asking if Sheridan knows about your plans for her father. I mean ... you guys are best friends, right? I would think it would be hard to hide something of that magnitude from a best friend."

"Who are you?" Rebecca looked bewildered. "Am I supposed to know who you are? Did Charles send you?"

That was an interesting reaction. "Last time I checked, Charles was still at the Beachcomber Resort being the world's biggest tool. That probably means he's overcompensating for a small tool, but I digress. I haven't heard about him leaving town yet and I'm most certainly not here on his behalf."

Now I was certain that the emotion I saw flitting across Rebecca's face was fear. "You saw him? Did you talk to him? Is he still angry with me? He left me a really angry message earlier, telling me I was an idiot and he didn't like my new attitude and wanted to break up. I've been trying to get him on the phone ever since, but he refuses to pick up."

Whoops! That was probably my fault. Ah, well. Rebecca was young. She would get over it ... as long as she wasn't a murderer. "You're better off without him."

"How can you say that?"

"Because he's a jerk. What's worse is that he knows he's a jerk and expects everyone to swallow it because they think he has money. The thing is, you know he doesn't have nearly as much money as he pretends. That begs the question, why are you still hanging around to take his abuse if you know he doesn't have money? You're clearly not in it for love."

"Am I on camera?" Rebecca darted her head from left to right, her eyes scanning the bushes and trees. "Is this for a reality show or something?"

"No. I really want to know if Sheridan knows about you and her father."

Rebecca slowly shook her head. "No. She doesn't know. Why would I tell her? She wouldn't take it well. In fact, she'd be royally ticked off. I'll have to hide for weeks once she finds out the truth."

"And what truth is that?" I prodded. "The one in which you only started dating her father because you wanted to break up his marriage or the one in which you want to get your hands on his money — money that should legitimately pass to her — and steal from her legacy?"

Rebecca wasn't a very good actress. She didn't even bother

to hide how flabbergasted she was. "I don't think I want to continue this discussion."

"I'm fine with that." I really wasn't, but it wasn't as if I could wrestle her to the ground and force her to give me answers. I'd end up in cuffs if I tried that, and Augie might be the one slapping them into place. "You don't have to answer my questions. I was merely curious. You can wait until you hit the mainland and the media there starts following you around looking for answers."

Rebecca worked her jaw, but no sound came out as her eyes widened.

"You really thought no one knew, didn't you?" I couldn't help being disappointed. "Everyone knows, Rebecca. The staff at the resort has been filled in on everything. They were warned to keep you and Blair Whitney apart should trouble arise."

Rebecca found her voice. "How do you know that?"

"I'm a busybody and I track things down. That's what I do. Once I tripped over Blair's body I had to find out more information. That led me straight to you. I have to ask: Did you kill her? You obviously knew about the life insurance policy. Did you kill her because you thought it was the easiest way to clear a path to Charles?"

"Of course not!" Rebecca practically screeched. "I would never kill Blair. She was like a mother to me sometimes ... sure, they were very rare times, but still sometimes."

Ugh. I don't think she thought that statement through. "If Blair was a mother figure, does that mean Charles is a father figure?"

"Don't be gross." Rebecca's temper flared to life. "I don't need this from you. I really don't. You're nobody. I don't have to talk to you."

"Then don't talk to me. I'm not forcing you. Like I said, I was curious. You're leaving tomorrow and I thought I would take a shot at getting answers. Trust me when I say that the people asking questions on the mainland will be a lot tougher than me. You should prepare yourself."

"And you should bite me." Rebecca's eyes flashed with something I couldn't quite identify. It looked like anger but felt like fear. "I'm done talking to you."

"Okay." I was ready to turn and leave, but the sight of Swoops gliding overhead stilled me.

Incoming. Incoming.

I had no idea what that was supposed to mean. "What's incoming?"

"I said I was done talking to you," Rebecca snapped. "I'm so done I ... ." She didn't get a chance to finish. Her jaw went slack and her eyes rolled back in her head. Then she was falling ... and fast ... and she hit the pavement with a sickening thud.

I remained rooted to my spot. "What the heck was that?"

Incoming!

Nineteen

I like to fancy myself fast on the uptake.

When I go to a movie that's billed as having a twist ending, I almost always figure it out early. The same with books.

When someone is trying to manipulate me, I see it coming long before the final move.

When one of my witchy sisters is out to play a prank, I almost always figure it out before public embarrassment becomes an issue.

This time I didn't see it coming. Even when Rebecca slumped to the ground I couldn't wrap my head around what was happening. It only got worse when I saw the figure standing behind where Rebecca had stood, her chest heaving and a rock clutched in her hand.

"I really can't believe I had to do this a second time," Sheridan announced, her demeanor calm. "I thought once would be enough. Clearly I wasn't thinking far enough ahead. Whew!"

I jolted at her high-pitched grunt at the end of the statement. "You?" It was a stupid question but I could think of nothing else to say. "You did this? I don't understand why."

As if realizing she wasn't alone for the first time, Sheridan gave me an extended once over. "Who are you?"

"Um ... ."

"I've seen you before." Sheridan pursed her lips. "Remind me where."

"I'm the one who stumbled over your mother's body." I saw no reason to lie. "You probably saw me that day because I was with the medical examiner and security."

"No, that's not it." Sheridan shook her head. "Where else might I have seen you?"

"I was out by the mud pit today when Augie hurried you and your probably dead friend away because of the smell." I wanted to nudge Rebecca with my foot, but that would mean moving closer to Sheridan. I was pretty sure I could take her – she wasn't large, after all – but I didn't want to risk it until I came up with a plan.

"Augie?" Sheridan made a face. "Wait, you're talking about August Taylor? The security guy? He's really cute. Is he single?"

"I have no idea. You'll have to ask him."

"Maybe I will." Sheridan didn't drop the rock, instead making a clucking sound with her tongue as she shook her head. "Even so, that's not where I recognize you from." She snapped her fingers after another moment of contemplation. "I know. You sang karaoke at that bar the other night. You shook your bottom with that guy."

"Augie."

"Was that him?" Sheridan didn't look convinced. "I thought he looked better earlier today than he did that night."

"That's probably because he was drunk the night we sang."

"Maybe." Sheridan seemed as if she was giving it real thought before she returned to reality. "So we have a problem. You saw what I did to Rebecca and I don't think I can just let you walk away and tell the police what you saw."

"Probably not." Her easygoing nature turned my stomach. She had to be deranged or something. "Have you ever been in a mental hospital?"

The question would've caught a normal person off guard. Sheridan was pretty far from a normal person. "Just that one – okay, two – times. The second time was really a mistake. I didn't kill the neighbor's dog. I paid someone else to do it. I should've gotten credit for thinking outside the box."

"Right." I risked a glance at Tut as he slowly padded across the parking lot. He didn't seem to be in a hurry, but he clearly knew where he was going. "So why did you kill your mother?"

"I should think that's obvious. My father lost most of his money in the economic downturn. I always believed I'd be able to live off my trust fund forever, but he tapped into that last year and now it's almost gone. We needed an influx of cash."

"We?" Every time I thought I understood where this was going I realized I couldn't possibly grasp all of it. "You and your father are in this together?"

"It had to be done." Sheridan stated matter-of-factly. "We talked about it. We both agreed that we needed the money. We also agreed it would be best for the accident to happen away from home."

I figured out the rest of it quickly. "You wanted to make it look like an accident. You thought people would believe your mother tripped and fell, hitting her head on one of the rocks."

"My mother was a functioning alcoholic and pill-head. She often wandered around in a daze. We were out here together that night. I led her away from the main building and even tried to trip her twice, but somehow she managed to stay on her feet.

"She was a babbler when she was lit, and she was going on and on about Rebecca as we walked," she continued. "I had to talk her into bringing Rebecca in the first place, of course. I needed someone to blame in case someone didn't believe the accident hypothesis. My mother was not happy about Rebecca coming, and she was especially not happy about Lena tagging along. There was nothing I could do about it, though."

"So, you wanted it to look like an accident but thought ahead enough to bring your father's mistress along," I mused. "That's almost diabolical."

"I knew we needed a scapegoat. I thought my father would put up a fight when I told him the second part of my plan. But he was fine with it. Truth be told, I think he was a little tired of Rebecca and all of her crap. If she could've gone to prison in the same breath as we unloaded Mom that would've been the best of both worlds."

She was cold hearted. I had to give her that. She didn't seem bothered at all by what she'd done. "So why go after Rebecca now?" I was genuinely curious. "A second accident isn't going to look good to the investigating officers."

"No. But there won't be a second body. Rebecca is simply going to disappear."

"Thus giving the cops an obvious suspect to focus on," I supplied. "That's smart."

"I graduated with top honors." Sheridan's smirk was bone chilling. "My father is on his way. He's going to help me dispose of Rebecca – he rented a boat and we're going to pull a *Dexter* – and then we'll be home free."

"It sounds like you've got it all planned out."

"We do."

"Except for one thing," I added. "You've yet to share what you plan to do with me."

"I should think that's rather obvious." Sheridan tightened her grip on the rock. "You're going to have to go missing with Rebecca."

"And how will you explain that?"

Sheridan shrugged. "I have no intention of ever mentioning you. Maybe the police will think you caught Rebecca doing something and she had to kill you to get away. That could be a good inciting incident for her to run. Yeah ... I like it."

"Inciting incident?"

"I watch a lot of lawyer shows. That's how I put this all together."

Somehow I saw that coming. "You're going to have to take me out for all of this to come to fruition. You know I won't go along willingly, right?"

"I don't expect you to." As if on cue, a set of headlights hit the parking lot. Sheridan didn't turn in that direction, but the corners of her lips curved in anticipation. "Here comes my backup now."

"Your father."

"Yup. We're about to be rich again. That's a great motivating factor."

"Well ... awesome."

"I'm sorry it has to go down this way." Sheridan seemed sincere. "You were simply in the wrong place at the wrong time. It's not personal."

Oh, that's where she was wrong. "It's very personal. It's been personal since I tripped over your mother's body. It's been personal since you whacked that poor, dim bulb friend of yours over the head. It's been personal since ... geez, you're all kinds messed up, aren't you?"

Sheridan didn't answer, instead widening her smile at the

sound of a vehicle door slamming shut. "Over here," she called loudly enough for someone close to hear.

He's coming. Run now.

Swoops flew in low enough to grab some of Sheridan's hair and distract her. She screeched, causing whoever was walking in the parking lot to pick up his pace and start running. It also allowed me an opening. Instead of fleeing toward the parking lot, which was illuminated but full of danger, I turned and bolted into the woods that led back to my house.

"Get it off of me!" Sheridan bellowed as she flailed her hands in an attempt to beat back Swoops. "Dad!"

I looked over my shoulder long enough to meet Charles Whitney's furious glare. For one brief moment I thought he would let me go. The smart thing would've been to pack up Sheridan and run. That was clearly wishful thinking, because Whitney increased his pace to a sprint when he realized what was happening.

Run!

Swoops was beside himself as he doubled his attack on Sheridan.

Don't look back!

For once I followed instructions without putting up a fuss.

ONCE I DISAPPEARED INTO the tree line I knew that I had the advantage even though I was outnumbered. Swoops would keep Sheridan busy. I could count on him for that. My biggest problem was that I had no idea if Charles was armed.

"Come back here!" He was yelling, so either he didn't understand how sound carried or he simply didn't care about being caught. Perhaps his adrenaline was an equalizer of sorts and he'd gone temporarily insane. It was a possibility.

I waited until I was sure I was far enough ahead to lay a trap before I peeled off to the right and circled through a dense stand of trees, slowing my pace so Charles wouldn't hear my feet shuffling through the underbrush.

"Come back here, girl!" Charles appeared under the moonlight, his chest heaving. I could see him clearly through the branches. He looked frustrated. It was more than that, though. He looked murderous. His daughter was the killer, but she took her cues from him.

"Were you grooming Sheridan her whole life for this or did you merely take advantage of her mental issues to solve a problem?"

Charles snapped his head in my direction. He couldn't see me, but it was obvious he understood I had changed the game. "Why didn't you keep running?"

He was smarter than I originally thought. His inner danger alarm was probably pinging up a storm. A normal girl would've run for the road, not stopping until she found sanctuary or help. I backtracked and positioned myself so I was behind him. Sure, I was still under cover, but I was closer than he imagined.

"Why do you think?" I enjoyed turning him into the prey. Perhaps it was sick, but I loved the freaked-out look on his face. "Why didn't you leave things alone? You could've gotten away with it if you had."

"Sheridan had a good idea, and getting rid of Rebecca makes things easier. The play would've worked without a hitch if it hadn't been for you."

"Yeah, well, I've never been known for making things easier on people." I narrowed my eyes as Charles leaned over and grabbed a large branch from the ground. He used it to start poking between the trees. I was far enough back he couldn't reach me – at least not yet.

"Why are you even involved in this?"

"Does it really matter?" I whispered a quick spell to muffle my movements and slipped away from the first stand of trees and into a second. This one was even farther from Charles.

"It matters to me," Charles growled. "We had everything planned out. Don't you understand that? You're acting as if my wife was a good person, that her death was somehow a great loss. She was a drunk who disengaged from life long ago. Her death was no loss."

"I'm sure it was to her."

Charles jerked his shoulders so hard I thought he might have toppled to the side, swinging wildly to look toward my new hiding place. "How did you do that?"

"Do what?"

"You know. I ... why didn't you run?"

He was putting it together. Sure, he was a lot slower than he should've been given the fact that he was here to commit a murder, but things were starting to slip into place.

"Why did you kill your wife rather than divorce her? I'll answer your question if you answer mine."

Charles squeezed his face into a grimace as he clenched his hands into fists at his side. The good news was that he didn't appear to be armed. The bad was that he seemed to be getting increasingly irritated and ready to start throwing punches ... or maybe even that big branch he held.

"Come on," I prodded. "If you answer my question, I'll answer yours."

"Fine. Is that what you want?" Charles threw up one hand in frustration. "What's that saying? The needs of the many outweigh the needs of the few. That's the one. My needs outweighed Blair's needs. Sheridan's needs were more important, too. That might sound crass, but that's the way of the world."

"Wow!" I didn't think he'd be so blunt. I thought the

explanation would be convoluted, perhaps a way to paint himself as a victim. He didn't even care enough to come up with a lie. "You're pretty cold, huh? You seem proud of it, too."

"I'm a realist." Charles narrowed his eyes as he stared directly at the spot I stood in five seconds earlier. I'd managed to move again without tipping him off. I was nowhere near where he thought I was. "I held up my end of the bargain. It's time for you to do the same. Why didn't you run? Why aren't you calling for help? Why aren't you screaming?"

All good questions for which I had a simple answer. I stepped out of my new hiding place and smirked at Charles' back. "Because I'm not afraid of you."

"What the ... ?"

Charles moved to swivel, but I pinned him in place, unleashing a burst of magic that turned him into a human Popsicle. I thought about circling him, allowing him to see my face before I finished him off, but that was a little too petty for my taste. I was trying to turn that new leaf, after all. Heck, I was debating dating Augie, for crying out loud. I was a whole new witch.

That didn't mean I could let him go.

"You're going to jail, Charles." I lifted my hands and pressed my eyes shut, feeding on the wind as it started to whip. "So is Sheridan, although she's nutty enough she might make a stop at a mental health facility first. All that money you were trying to claim through Blair's death will go for lawyers now. Is that what you wanted?"

Charles couldn't answer because of the spell, but he let loose an angry grunt. It promised mayhem if he got loose. There was no way I was going to let that happen.

"Perhaps you should get a dose of your own medicine, huh?" My braid smacked the side of my face as the wind increased. "I need a little fun of my own after this crap factory of a week. I guess I might as well start with you."

I released the first spell at the exact moment the second captured Charles and pitched him forward, pushing him to his knees as he fought the magic. "What is going on? I ... what is happening? I'm going to make you pay for this."

"Shh," I admonished. "It's time for a nap. I'll wake you when the police arrive."

"There's still a way out of this," Charles barked. "I can give you some of the insurance payout. You don't have to do this."

He was wrong. This was exactly what I had to do.

"Have a nice night, Charles. I'll see you in a little bit."

I let the magic fly and then stood back to watch Charles Whitney face what he so richly deserved.

Twenty

I was still standing next to Charles' prone body twenty minutes later when I heard running in the forest.

Tut, who waited with me, twitched his ears. "Help is coming."

I knew who it was before I even saw his shadow. "Augie."

"I'll leave you to it." Tut's tail slashed as he moved to the other side of the small clearing. "Don't worry about reporting back to the home office. I'll handle that for you."

I knew it! "Go ahead, tattletale."

"I'm going to tell them you managed to balance both sides of your life for a change." Tut disappeared into the underbrush. "Perhaps you're showing growth after all. Try not to make a fool of yourself with August Taylor. It will ruin your perfect day if you do."

I managed to contain my temper, but just barely. I jerked my head to the right when Augie came crashing through the trees, pulling up short when he saw me and leaning over to catch his breath.

"You're okay," he wheezed out, pressing his side as if to

ease a stitch. "I wasn't sure. I thought ... ." His eyes landed on Charles. "Is that who I think it is?"

"Charles Whitney," I volunteered, bobbing my head. "It seems he was working with his daughter. They plotted together to kill Blair and then they decided to add Rebecca to the mix." *Rebecca!* I'd almost forgotten about her. "Is she ... alive?"

Augie nodded as he studied my face. I wasn't sure how I was supposed to react — I'd used my magic to take out a murderous human, after all — and I could only hope he thought I was in shock. That would be my best defense.

"She's alive," Augie confirmed, his expression unreadable. "The paramedics transported her to the hospital. She regained consciousness as they were loading her onto the gurney but didn't seem to know who attacked her."

Uh-oh. "It was Sheridan. I ... did she get away?" The idea of joining a search to find that nutjob filled me with dread. "Maybe we should start putting together teams."

Augie held up his hand to still me. "We got her. She wasn't far from Rebecca. She was cowering behind a bush. She kept waving her hands around, as if warding off an attack. She admitted to everything if we agreed to save her from the attacking bat ... something we didn't see."

Swoops. "Oh, well ... ."

"That's how I knew you were in trouble," Augie continued, barely taking a breath as he barreled forward. "You're the only person I know with an attack bat. Sheridan said she was talking to a woman and that woman ordered her bat to attack and then she took off into the woods."

I was affronted. "I didn't order Swoops to attack." As if I'd need a bat to protect me from the likes of Sheridan. "He did it on his own."

Augie chuckled, the sound catching me off guard. "I love that you're somehow offended by that. Does it matter? The more we let her talk, the more Sheridan basically handcuffed herself. When she mentioned her father's part in everything, and said he chased a pretty blonde into the woods ... well, I knew."

"I'm fine." I gestured toward Charles and wrinkled my nose. "He's going to have a bit of a headache."

"I figured." Augie took an uncertain step toward me. "Did he touch you?"

"No. Well, I guess a little. But I managed to get behind him and slam his head into a tree to make sure he was down. I'm pretty sure I did ten times more damage to him than he did to me. He only scratched me."

"Let me see." Augie closed the distance between us and grabbed the hand I held up. There was a thin scratch across my knuckles. "That doesn't look so bad."

"I said I was fine." I forced a smile for his benefit. "I'm really tired, though."

"I don't blame you." Augie gave my hand a squeeze before releasing it. "Um ... I'll take care of Mr. Whitney. You'll probably have to fill out a police report tomorrow so they have everything on record. If you're tired, you can go home. I'll handle the rest of this."

It was a tempting offer ... and one I needed to take. I was exhausted from letting loose two huge bursts of magic in one day. I needed sleep. "I'll contact the police department first thing in the morning."

"Okay." Augie looked as if he wanted to say more. I hoped he would hold off for at least twenty-four hours. I still needed to think things through where he was concerned. "Go home and rest, Skye. I'll catch up with you tomorrow."

I was so relieved I almost kissed him. I thought better of it, though. "Great." I moved toward the familiar path and stilled. "Augie, thanks for coming to my rescue."

Augie's chuckle was soft. "You didn't need me to rescue you."

"No, but it's still nice you tried. I mean ... you showed up. That's the most important thing, right?"

"Definitely."

"I'll see you tomorrow."

"I'm looking forward to it."

AFTER TEN HOURS OF sleep and a huge breakfast of corned beef hash and eggs (I thought Swoops deserved it after his showing the previous evening) I spent two hours at the police station answering questions and filling out reports. Charles and Sheridan were both behind bars – Charles showing no lingering effects at having his head smacked against a tree – and they couldn't scramble fast enough to point the finger at one another. Sadly, I thought there was a chance Charles might get off with a lighter sentence than he deserved because he could claim he was trying to protect his crazy-pants daughter, but it wasn't something I could dwell on.

Once finished there, I stopped at the coffee shop long enough to grab a big dose of caffeine, and then I headed to the newspaper office. It was almost lunch and I was considering ordering something to be delivered. Instead, I found a blanket spread on the ground in front of the building ... and a smiling Augie sitting on it as he waited for me to join him.

I came to a full stop ten feet away. "What are you doing here?"

"Well, I've been giving it some thought." Augie kept his hands busy by removing things from the picnic basket to his right. "At first I believed the right thing to do was to give you time to think about what you wanted."

Hmm. "And you've changed your mind now?"

Augie bobbed his head. "If I give you too much time you'll find a way to talk yourself out of this. I don't want that. I want to give it a try."

"And what if it doesn't work? I mean, let's face it, if two people were ever destined to muck up a situation, it's us."

Augie snickered, the sound low and throaty. "That's true, but I still want to try."

"Why?"

"Because the idea of not trying is worse than trying and failing."

I'd pretty much come to the same conclusion myself, although I wasn't sure I wanted to admit it because that would be like rewarding him for his cheeky behavior. "Well ... I still might not be done thinking about it."

I finished crossing to him and tucked my legs under me as I sat on the blanket, leaning to the side so I could peer into the basket. "Is that pasta salad?"

"From the market. I know it's your favorite."

"How do you know that?"

"I know you better than you think." Augie's smile was so charming it melted something inside of me. "I want you to say yes, that you're willing to at least try."

"Why do you need me to say it?"

"Because you're a woman of your word." Augie was earnest. "If you say you'll try, I can believe it. It may fall apart down the line, but I know you'll try. You always follow through."

He needed to hear the words. I could understand that. Still, I wanted to delay the inevitable. "If we do this, how will it work?"

"What do you mean?"

"I mean ... how will it work?" I repeated. "Will we go to restaurants and bars together? Will we hold hands and skip through meadows? Will there be overnight visits? Are you going to complain about my bat? Are you going to give me crap for trying to sucker information out of Dylan? Are you going to, like ... kiss me in public?"

Augie's face filled with amusement. "Your head is a busy place, isn't it?"

He had no idea. "I just want some clarification."

"Okay. Fair enough." He nodded. "We'll definitely go to restaurants and bars together. We kind of already started that last night. It was fine. Actually, it was better than fine. I enjoyed myself.

"I can't really see us skipping through meadows because neither one of us is the skipping sort," he continued. "I think holding hands will be something that happens on a date-by-date basis, mostly contingent on your mood."

I stirred. "Why my mood?"

"Because you're moodier than me and pretending otherwise is a waste of time."

He was right. "Continue."

"I think I'm looking forward to the overnight visits most of all, but they're not something I'm keen to rush," Augie supplied. "I think we'll know when it's the right time for that. I will probably complain about the bat because it's odd and strange to have a pet bat."

"He distracted Sheridan last night and made it so I wasn't outnumbered," I reminded him.

"Which means I'll probably end up liking him." Augie grinned. "I will still give Dylan grief for giving you information. I have a job to do. So do you. That aspect of our relationship probably won't change."

That didn't sound so bad. "Well, I guess that's fair enough. We can give it a try."

Augie's lips did a little dance, as if he didn't want me to know he was secretly pleased by the words. I felt his excitement, though. Oddly enough, I shared it.

"That's good, but I wasn't done."

"Oh." I sucked in a breath when Augie leaned so close our lips almost touched. "What else were you going to say?" My head felt light and giddy. It was ridiculous I could still feel this way at my age ... and yet I did.

"I hadn't gotten to the kissing part yet," Augie said. "You wanted to know if I was going to kiss you in public."

"Right." My heart pounded harder. "Are you?"

"What do you think?" Augie didn't wait for me to answer, instead slowly pressing his lips against mine.

My first instinct was mortification. What if someone saw? We wouldn't hear the end of it for weeks. When he deepened the kiss, though, and my fingertips and toes turned tingly, I decided I didn't care about any of that.

What's a little mortification, after all? There was every chance Augie might be worth every moment of discomfort. I was looking forward to finding out.